"This unexpected appearance of yours is nothing, of course, to do with my recent divorce?" Chance asked softly

Rosalind saw his hand lifting, a finger preparing to touch her mouth. And she was so stunned by his revelation that she was unable to avoid the contact. It evoked a response powerful enough to make her quiver from head to toe. She never knew her moan of need was coming or she would have stopped it.

"I thought so," he muttered.

Childhood in Portsmouth meant grubby knees, flying pigtails and happiness for *SARA WOOD*. Poverty drove her from typist and seaside landlady to teacher, till writing finally gave her the freedom her Romani blood craved. Happily married, she has two handsome sons. Richard is married, calm, dependable, drives tankers; Simon is a roamer—silversmith, roofer, welder, always with beautiful girls. Sara lives in the Cornish countryside. Her glamorous writing life alternates with her passion for gardening which allows her to be carefree and grubby again!

Books by Sara Wood

Don't miss any of our special offers. Write to us at the following address for information on our newest releases.

Harlequin Reader Service
U.S.: 3010 Walden Ave., P.O. Box 1325, Buffalo, NY 14269
Canadian: P.O. Box 609, Fort Erie, Ont. L2A 5X3

SARA WOOD

Southern Passions

Harlequin Books

TORONTO • NEW YORK • LONDON
AMSTERDAM • PARIS • SYDNEY • HAMBURG
STOCKHOLM • ATHENS • TOKYO • MILAN
MADRID • WARSAW • BUDAPEST • AUCKLAND

ISBN 0-373-11715-9

SOUTHERN PASSIONS

CHAPTER ONE

HORIZONTAL in the barber's chair, he lay with his arrogant chin buried beneath a froth of white foam and the best Irish linen draped over his torso. Smooth, seamless New Orleans jazz drifted across the exclusive salon and he listened to it with evident pleasure, smoke-dark lids closed blissfully.

Rosalind felt a flutter of nerves and contemplated the cut-throat razor in the barber's hand. It was late afternoon. Time for Chance Broussard Decatur to get that sexy dark jaw shaven, so that he could nuzzle the delicate skin of some sweet Southern belle. Her expression hardened. She had to see this through.

'Hi there. How y'all doin'? Isn't this a great day, ma'am?'

Still in the doorway, she kept her blue eyes fixed on the languidly reclining figure of the man she despised most in the whole wide world.

'Oh, great,' she murmured.

But first she'd have to confront Chance. The courage to do so was draining away from her the longer she stood beneath the gently whirring ceiling-fan.

'Come for Mr Chance?' hazarded the assistant, following her gaze.

'I'll say,' she answered grimly, and strode forwards. Sure now of herself, dressed to kill, to impress, to sock Chance Decatur between the eyes with her self-assurance, she smiled her sweetest at the head barber—who else would be shaving an aristocratic oil baron?—and took the razor from the man's hand. 'Let me,' she whispered in the man's ear. 'He'll be so surprised.'

5

The man hesitated, torn between snatching the razor away and letting her have her own way. She tried to look regally amazed at his temerity. Deferentially he inclined his head and Rosalind knew he was a little in awe of the Decatur penchant for beautiful women and disinclined to upset this particular one. Of course, he'd also summed up the quality of her expensive outfit that whispered power and authority: the purpose-bought Givenchy suit in a soft, figure-enhancing green.

Rosalind knew she looked better and classier and icier than at any time in her life. No torrid New Orleans summer was going to ruin her professional make-up or the smoothness of her sleekly coiled dark chignon. All joyful curls rigorously tamed. All jitters under control. The razor hovered by his ear.

Quietly she placed her handbag on the marble table beside the aromatic French coffee and obligatory square doughnuts, those heavenly, fattening, sugared *beignets*. Maybe his figure had deteriorated. A glance at the flat, starched-crisp linen which covered Chance's chest and stomach told her otherwise. His hair was still as black as pitch to match his heart and his skin the colour of pale molasses to match his treacle-laden tongue.

Rosalind took a deep breath and her beautifully de-fined red lips narrowed into an ominous line. She reached over his oblivious, vulnerable body, frowning at the small leap of her normally steady pulses. Her thigh came into contact with his hand which loosely lay on the leather arm of the barber's chair and she noticed an involuntary stiffening of his muscles.

He knows that's a woman's thigh! she thought in amazement. Quickly her hand flew out and she laid the wicked blade against his cheek just as his eyes flickered open and tried to focus. Her stomach took a trip all on its own to the ground floor of the building, several storeys below. Chance Decatur had eyes as fatal as a Mississippi swamp.

'Move an inch and half your face will hit the floor,' she whispered softly, smiling for the benefit of the discreetly busy barbers, whose eyes kept shifting to the mirror in total fascination.

'Sweetheart, *you* move an inch, and all my blood-pressure'll hit the ceiling,' Chance murmured. A Southern drawl with a French accent, backed by sultry New Orleans jazz. What could be more seductive?

Disconcerted because he wasn't petrified with fear, Rosalind saw the impertinent dark eyes honing in on the open V of her neckline. By her leaning forwards, her perfectly proper jacket had become revealing, indicating the presence of the voluptuous hills of her breasts, apparently eager to offer themselves to him. With a mouth pinched to show her disdain, she moved back slightly but increased the pressure on his cheek. His chest swelled beneath the linen; other than that, he showed no alarm and she wondered at his confidence.

'Where's Annie?' she asked in a conversational tone.

Chance's eyes narrowed. 'Ros?' he whispered huskily. '*Ros*?'

'Rosalind,' she corrected coolly.

His jaw dropped in disbelief, then he grinned, his wicked, woman-melting grin, the sort the pirate Jean Lafitte would have been proud of. 'Real sassy assistants they hire nowadays,' he drawled.

Goaded, Rosalind promptly swept some of the shaving foam across his open mouth, maliciously enjoying his spluttering. But she'd relaxed her guard and before she knew what was happening her wrist was being surrounded by the ruthlessly tightening steel of Chance's cruel fingers.

'You brute!' she gasped, wincing from the pain.

'Sister, you ain't seen nuttin' yet,' he muttered, in a heavy imitation of jazz-cellar drawl.

The razor dropped to the floor with a clatter, Chance dragged the linen cloth across his soapy mouth then rammed down hard on the chair's hydraulic lever and suddenly Rosalind found herself flat on her stomach. Balancing precariously on Chance.

'You're taking liberties!' she glared, her eyes inches from his.

'Do something stupid again and I will,' he said menacingly, his chest inflated with anger, the hard, hot muscles beneath his shirt pressing into her crushed breasts. 'If you're wondering what we do next,' he drawled in husky appreciation, 'I have a suggestion or two.'

'I don't give public performances,' she said coldly.

'One hold, one submission,' he muttered, his eyes hard.

A quiver of fear ran through Rosalind. She'd made him look a fool in front of the whole barber's shop—and he was far too important a man to take that kind of treatment and not go for revenge. She knew how ruthless he could be with his enemies...

Far too close to the cruel face and its blazingly angry eyes, she relentlessly composed herself. As much as any woman could, who lay full length on a man as virile and as threatening as Chance Decatur.

'Where's Annie?' she asked, as if nothing had happened. Not even the awakening of her whole body, outside, inside...

A small smile curved the high corners of his impossibly sensual lips. 'You frozen bitch!' he said, softly mocking.

'Mr Chance, sir——!' broke in the barber, nervous at the temerity of remonstrating with such an influential man. The Decaturs went back to the French Revolution and they'd only ever married their own kind; two hundred years of pure-bred aristocrats. That counted in Louisiana.

For a moment, the glittering eyes left Rosalind's. 'Sure, Pedro. We'll fight elsewhere. I'll find a nearby swamp. This is fighting dirty.'

The chair folded itself into a chair again and Chance ended up holding Rosalind on his lap where she sat with great dignity as if it didn't matter that she could feel the alarming heat of Chance's strongly muscled thighs burning into her. Dear heaven, she thought in alarm as he released his grip on her arms. He wants me. He finds this exciting.

In one elegant movement, she rose from his lap and accusingly massaged her sore wrists. 'We're not fighting,' she said evenly. 'You're going to tell me where Annie is, and then I'm going to leave.'

'How the devil did you find me here?' he asked.

In perfect rhythm with the blues now throbbing through the cool salon, Chance began to strop a fresh razor with menacing thoroughness. Rosalind's heart thudded faster. But he merely leaned forwards to give himself a hasty shave, the sharp blade flicking expertly over his even-toned skin. Considering the circumstances, his control was astounding.

'Luck. I'd been pestering your secretary for a long time, one way or another. As I left, I overheard a conversation in your office,' she answered.

'If I thought anyone had told you my private movements, I'd fire them.'

'Your dragon guards your lair well,' retorted Rosalind. 'You always had a good line of defence against persistent women.'

He smiled and crooked an eyebrow at her. 'Of course. You and Annie helped to keep my women out of my hair when I was working, didn't you? It left the way clear for you two, of course,' he murmured, carefully sliding the razor over the soft skin above his sultry Gallic mouth. 'I forgot to be wary of the women *inside* the barricades.'

She glowered, still surprised by his calm. Even if his current secretary had passed on her messages, her arrival out of the blue must have been a shock. They hadn't seen one another in eight years and she was far from the green-as-grass girl he'd known when she and Annie had taken up her American pen-friend's suggestion and gone to work for him. And fallen for him, head-over-heels. He must recognise her current air of self-assurance, he must be surprised. Yet his hand never faltered in its quick, deft movements.

His extraordinary indifference emphasised the fact that everything that had happened between them was of no importance to him at all. She choked back the swell of misery inside her. 'Annie,' she prompted.

His eyes met hers in the mirror, dark and enigmatic. 'I don't know where she is,' he answered casually.

Rosalind couldn't believe her ears. 'You don't know? You don't *know*? Good grief, Annie's your wife!' she cried indignantly. And your child, she wanted to scream, to take his shoulders and shake the truth out of him. Where is she?

'I've still no idea.'

He shrugged his careless French shrug, more interested in checking the smoothness of his jaw. Time stood still. Rosalind tried not to remember when she'd seen him do that before, but her pulses quickened nevertheless, leaving her short of breath as his hand slid over the smooth, flawless bronze skin.

Deliberately inflicting self-torture, she told herself that hundreds of women had watched him shave after a steamy night in his arms. They'd desired that blatantly erotic mouth and had wondered how long they'd have to wait before it was again branding every inch of their bodies. The contempt soon returned to swamp her sentimental memories and she fixed him with a sceptical look.

'That's ridiculous——' she began irritably.

'Don't you believe me?' he drawled. 'I'm not kidding you. Annie could be anywhere. Does it matter where? And,' he continued, checking his antique fob watch, 'if that's all, I have an appointment, so——'

'Your child,' interrupted Rosalind, her mind whirling with unnamed fears. She couldn't stop herself from asking, her whole being concentrated on the one vital question. 'Melanie...' She swallowed. 'What have you done with your daughter?'

Chance slanted a curious glance at her. She stood rigidly holding her breath, two pink spots high on her cheeks, her blue eyes wide with apprehension. 'Thrashed her within an inch of her life and sold her to slavers. What's it to you?' he asked grimly.

He pushed past her trembling body and dealt out dollar bills to the shampoo boys and the barber with the extravagance of gesture she well remembered.

She wanted to throw something, to let out the hysteria mounting inside her. Instead, she stalked angrily in his wake. 'I'm Melanie's godmother and Annie's my friend!' Rosalind said sharply, not caring that New Orleans society would be discussing this over their mint juleps in a few hours. 'I—I have a responsibility to my godchild. I haven't heard from Annie——'

She felt the woosh of the glass swing door coming towards her as Chance strode through it and insolently let it go in her face. Catching it, she stormed after him on her spiky heels, bought for authority rather than running after men.

People were watching, but then people always had watched Chance when he began to move. It was like seeing a lithe animal prowling in its natural habitat, limbs fluid and sensuous, body swaggering a little from side to side, dark head held proudly and eyes alert for any opportunity.

Ignoring her completely, he flowed into the lift, managing to give several young women the glad eye at the same time. His wicked coal-dark eyes mocked Rosalind as she tried to beat the closing lift doors.

'Hold it for the little lady!' drawled a Texan voice. A blonde giant slammed Desperate Dan fists between the steel doors and prised them open.

'Thank you,' gasped Rosalind gratefully.

'My pleasure, ma'am,' said the Texan in admiration.

Despite her concern, her face relaxed a little and for a while she was coaxed into conversation by the pleasantly friendly Texan who seemed eager to escort her around New Orleans.

'My card,' he said. 'If you want to hit the high spots, call me. Been a treat talkin' to an English lady like you. Have a nice day, now.'

'Thank you.' Not wanting to hurt his feelings, Rosalind took the card and smiled. Her eyes flickered over to the silent Chance.

The pleasure left her face. They were alone. He was leaning against the padded side of the lift, his whole body tense and threatening. A tiny nerve began to throb in her temple. She knew she was being reckless in deliberately pestering him and common sense told her to stop the lift and run like crazy.

'Well, little lady,' he said, quietly mocking. 'Are you going to call that overstuffed Texan steer and hit the high spots?'

Her chin lifted. 'What I do is my business and no one else's,' she said frostily.

Chance scowled, two deep creases pinching grooves between his black brows. 'You've changed. Joined the hell-cats by the looks of it. My memories of you are shattered, Rosalind.'

'I'm delighted to hear that,' she muttered. The last thing she wanted was for Chance to know she was still soft and vulnerable.

'What are you here for?' he asked suspiciously. 'Why stay away for eight solid years and then return at *this* particular time?'

Rosalind closed down the fear that had haunted her, night after night, until it had reached mammoth proportions. Going through Annie's letters again and reading between the lines, she'd picked up vague hints of Chance's absence due to work. Work or women? And the letters had seemed increasingly agitated as if Annie was afraid of something.

Chance was so physical. Had his quick passion turned to irritation with a wife who was losing her looks? Annie kept complaining how fat she was.

'I came because I'm worried sick about my friend,' she said quietly. 'Ever since I left New Orleans we've kept in contact. Yet I've heard nothing from her for the last six months.'

'So ring her.'

'I have. I've telephoned the plantation dozens of times and the maid tells me she's not there. I leave messages and get no reply, nor any answer to my letters,' she said, her voice shaking slightly. 'My God, Chance,' she said in a husky whisper, 'if you've upset, or harmed her in any way——'

He swore under his breath. The lift stopped on the ground floor. Chance strode out, his face thunderous, his muscles no longer loose and easy but tensed as tightly as a knotted rope. Her fears escalating, she had to break into a half-run to keep up, as he seared a path around the atrium's fountains and across the vast shopping mall.

'I won't get involved in this. I have no interest in her,' he snapped, when she tugged at his arm urgently. 'My role in her life consists of paying the bills.'

'You heartless devil!' breathed Rosalind, quite aghast at his indifference. 'Annie loves you! How can you suggest she looks on you just as a provider? She's always wanted a family life, you know that. Heavens, I wonder sometimes why you ever married——'

He stopped abruptly and she bumped into him, leaping back immediately at the savage fury in his hot eyes. 'Well now,' he snarled. 'Isn't that interesting? So do I.'

Rosalind winced. Annie had never given her any hint that the marriage was foundering. 'Where is she? What have you done with her? I'll keep harassing you, Chance Decatur,' she seethed, 'till I know the whereabouts of my friend and—and Melanie,' she faltered, her throat constricting.

'Save me from such a fate!' he muttered. 'As far as I know, Annie's at Sans Souci. I expect she hasn't answered your calls to the plantation because she's too busy out spending my money.'

'You've no right to talk of Annie with such contempt——'

'You damn haughty Englishwoman!' he snarled. 'She's earned it! I show contempt where it's due. Most women earn it, most women get it. So far I've found nothing honourable about any of you—which is why I don't swallow your story of sisterly love for an old friend. So level with me. I want the *real* reason you've come hounding me.'

Rosalind looked at him warily, seeing the scrolling scorn in the lines of his mouth, and she blanched. Oh, Annie! she cried in silent prayer, trying to stop her face from registering panic. You haven't told him our secret, please say you haven't. He'd throttle us both if he knew.

They stepped from the air-conditioned building into the steamy hot New Orleans street and it was like walking into a sauna. She used the few seconds of adjustment to gather together her few remaining rags of control. The moisture-laden air weighed heavily on her lungs and it gave her voice an excuse for being so breathless.

'I've told you the real reason,' she insisted hoarsely, deciding to bluff this out. 'I'm worried about the apparent disappearance of two people I care for.'

She pressed a handkerchief to her forehead and discovered that the humidity was already making her thick, glossy hair spring from the sophisticated coil into its natural curls around her face.

'Oh, yes?' Chance's imperious arm summoned a taxi. He turned and faced her, his expression harsh and cynical. 'This unexpected appearance of yours is nothing, of course, to do with my recent divorce?' he asked softly.

'Divorce?' she cried in horror.

Rosalind's lips remained parted in shock. Then she saw, as if in slow motion, Chance's hand lifting, a finger preparing to touch her mouth. And she was so stunned by his revelation that she was unable to step back to avoid the contact. The lightness of his touch on her soft, pliable mouth was deceptive. Because it evoked a response powerful enough to make her quiver from head to toe. His finger traced the high bow and swept contemptuously over the lush swelling scarlet, briefly, nerve-jerkingly, slipping a fraction inside to the moist inner part. And Rosalind never knew her moan of need was coming or she would have stopped it.

'I thought so,' he muttered. 'Get in.'

'What——?' She was bundled roughly into the car. Chance half fell against her, the weight of his body trapping her.

'Corner of Canal and Royal,' he snapped at the driver.

Then his arms went around her and his mouth was hard on hers, angry, destructive, his teeth clenched behind his cruel lips, his body taut with violence. Rosalind struggled angrily, fighting the reeling of her senses and upset at the cruel contrast with the kisses she'd once delighted in, tender, sweet and murmuring. She thought of the firm clasp of his hand when they had strolled in the moonlight along Moon Walk levée, gazing into each other's eyes. Young love. Tender, true, with the promise of an eternity together.

She gave a long, shuddering sob. 'Swine!' she whispered miserably.

His embrace tightened grimly. And she then remembered with a chilling shock that she wasn't dealing with a charming young man any more, but someone whose character had hardened and become brutalised after spending two years in prison.

That knowledge froze her. She became motionless, unresponsive, terrified out of her wits by Chance's irrational assault. Suddenly, he pushed himself away and flung himself into the opposite corner of the cab, his mood savage as ever.

'You aren't eager to fall into my arms,' he said without expression.

Rosalind was astounded. It was several seconds before she could bring herself to reply. 'Find me a one-eyed alligator with festering sores, and I'd choose him over you,' she snapped angrily. 'Let me out. Before I fling myself into the path of a streetcar and cause a scandal that even the Decatur millions won't hush up.'

He gave her a jaundiced look. 'That would be nothing to the rumours I've survived,' he said coldly. 'But I'll let you out if that's what you're pretending you want.' He told the driver to stop. 'If you run short of alligators, call me. But be sure you know what I'd expect from you.'

'What might that be?' she asked haughtily.

He leaned across her, smiling mockingly when she pressed back into the seat to avoid being touched, but he merely opened the door.

'Work it out for yourself. Just remember I'm a very, very hungry male and I take a lot of satisfying. Have a nice day,' he husked in her ear.

Rosalind stepped out, feeling the searing heat scorching her legs as she did so, and then it hit her whole body, sapping her strength. Or perhaps it was the effect of meeting Chance again. All this time she'd hoped that she'd been wrong about him, that her anxieties were unfounded. But she'd been right to sense from Annie's letters that Chance wasn't around as much as he ought to be. As before, his life was once again occupied only by work and women. Rosalind frowned. Judging by his attitude just now, his opinion of women was even lower than in the past.

Trembling, she stood in front of a plank house in St Charles Avenue and held on to the wrought-iron railings, watching the cab disappear from view, trying to come to terms with the fact that she'd known nothing about Chance's divorce.

It meant Annie and Melanie were on their own, unhappy, bewildered, needing comfort. Rosalind's heart went out to them and she supposed that her friend had been too traumatised by the divorce to contact her. But where had they gone?

Rosalind straightened. She'd blown it. Chance had been her one remaining link with Melanie and now he wouldn't dream of helping her. Her hand tightened on the spiked rail and she briefly enjoyed imagining the spike stuck in Chance's arrogant, over-sexed body. But for Melanie's sake, she might have to swallow her pride and beg for his help.

First, she tried the plantation a few times, but no one even answered the phone. She checked all the sources which might hold Annie's new address, but it seemed that she must have left New Orleans. That didn't leave her with much of a choice.

So she forced herself to ring Chance's office, her stomach churning at the thought of another confrontation, and managed to get through to his office after insisting it was a matter of life and death.

'Rosalind Baker, and I must speak to Mr Decatur urgently,' she told the guardian dragon haughtily.

'I'm sorry, Miss Baker, but he's not available.'

Rosalind seethed. Those were the very same words she and Annie had used to fob off pestering women during his working day. She hated being bracketed with his groupies.

'Then I'll leave a message. Tell Mr Decatur that either he sees me or I contact the Missing Persons Bureau,' she said grimly. 'You've got my number. Tell him to ring me.'

'Just a minute,' came the dragon's stilted tones. 'He might have come in.' It sounded, thought the oversensitive Rosalind, as if the dragon was used to female threats and knew when to surrender to them. After a long and agonising pause, the woman came back on the line. 'Mr Decatur says to go ahead and make a fool of yourself.'

Rosalind heard the click as the line was disconnected and she let out a groan. For a while she paced up and down her hotel room, plucking up courage, persuading herself that she had no alternative but to lure Chance from behind the barricades.

Loathing what she was doing, she called again, her fingers barely managing to dial the numbers. 'Rosalind Baker again.' She heard a click and began to panic. 'Hello? Can you hear me?'

'Oh, yes, Miss Baker,' said the dragon, sounding amused.

'Tell Mr Decatur...' She swallowed and tried again. 'Tell him I'll buy him lunch and we can talk about alligator wrassling,' she husked, her mouth dry. She waited impatiently, uncertain that she wanted him to accept.

'Sounds exciting. I'll pick you up in your hotel at one,' came Chance's mocking tones. 'Where are you?'

He'd been listening in! 'The—the Marriott,' she breathed, suddenly appalled at what she'd done. He'd made some crack earlier, about expecting something from her if she contacted him again. Rosalind groaned inwardly. She was laying herself on the line.

'Lobby bar, then,' he murmured. 'Be there. I don't wait for women. They wait for me. And wear something I can enjoy looking at. I'm breaking two appointments for this and you might as well make it worth my while.'

The line was disconnected and Rosalind was left bitterly regretting her rash offer. 'Rat!' she muttered to herself. 'Evil, arrogant rat!'

She spent the time inventing worse names for him and working herself up into a state of nervous tension wondering whether he would help her or not—and what it might cost her. As if she didn't know. She'd be treated like any other of his potential conquests: with cynical ruthlessness. She steeled herself to the ordeal. He was expecting sex but he'd have to settle for lunch. Parrying Chance's passes and perhaps fighting him off in a taxi was a small price to pay.

Because she'd give her life for Melanie.

She was early. She perched on the edge of one of the seats in the lobby lounge, nursing a daiquiri, and her huge blue eyes anxiously watched for him. And suddenly there he was, tall, perfectly groomed, wearing a cool sand suit that heightened the effect of his dark colouring.

His eyes went straight to her, his approving gaze setting her alight in an instant as he took in her fashionable black dress with its tightly fitting bodice and short, leg-revealing skirt. She'd taken him at his word, knowing she'd have to soften him up and get him talking. If she'd worn something prim he would have been quite capable of perversely turning on his heel and breaking their date. He liked his women to show willing and was too proud to waste time running after them.

Rosalind quivered with nerves at the long, devouring look, wondering if she'd chosen unwisely. But she had to persuade him to co-operate and she'd go to almost any lengths to know what had happened to Melanie.

The fear of permanently losing contact with the little girl had forced her into this situation. But she'd go through with it. If she wanted to trap an alligator, she had to use the right bait. She wriggled uncomfortably, quelling the rising panic. He could look. It wouldn't hurt her to feed his avid male eyes.

Slowly Chance ascended the short flight of stairs. Heads swivelled to look at him but he seemed unaware or too used to being admired, and strolled unconcernedly over to the chair in front of her. 'That's some dress. You are very beautiful, Rosalind,' he murmured.

She trembled at the unnerving warmth in his tone. 'Thank you,' she said, her face too stiff to smile.

'Blatant, cool and beautiful. You *are* up to something to go to such lengths. Do we thrash about together now, or after lunch?' he drawled, vastly amused by the situation.

'I've made it no secret that I want something from you——' she began evenly.

'Don't state the obvious,' he murmured. 'Get me a Dixie, will you?' he called to the hovering barmaid. He crossed one elegantly shod foot over the other. 'I know when I'm being stalked. You and Annie and that penfriend of yours...what was her name?'

'Josie,' she supplied grimly.

'Oh, yes. Well, you three didn't exactly hide your intentions. When pen-pal Josie wrote to you saying there were jobs vacant in my office, did she tell you about her boss?' he queried languidly. 'That I was fair game for any woman, that I was rich and available and up for grabs?'

She shuddered. 'No. You make it sound so——'

'Calculating?' he suggested.

'It was nothing of the kind and you're quite aware of that. Annie and I came over because we wanted to make a new beginning in a new country,' she said in a low tone.

'Oh, the ambition showed,' he drawled. 'You both tried so hard.'

Her eyes met his resentfully. 'We never wanted to be poor again. We wanted to make it on our own backs, not some man's. You know I'd had a terrible relationship with my stepmother. You know both our fathers were alcoholics and that Annie and I had clung together through the rough times. It's no crime to want more out of life than deceit and hardship.'

Chance was looking around the room, either to avoid eye-contact, or, more likely, to see if anyone more interesting had entered the lobby. Apparently they hadn't, because he gave her a glance from under his lashes of pure disbelief.

'You all did your best to get your sexy little bodies into my bed and your fingers on the Decatur fortune——'

'That's not true!' she said indignantly.

'No?' He leaned back, one arm along the back of the seat in a posture of insolent, brooding negligence. 'I was twenty. I'd been leading almost a monastic life and was just getting into my stride with the women of New Orleans when you three offered yourselves, one after the other, and then came back for more.'

'How dare you suggest such a thing? It wasn't like that and we didn't *offer* ourselves,' Rosalind said stiffly.

'Yes, you did. You were like the witches of Eastwick, plotting and brewing your spells,' he said caustically. 'You three women did everything together—shared an apartment, triple-dated, worked in the same office. First Annie threw herself at me——'

'You seduced her,' Rosalind corrected.

'Not at all. She made all the running, I was content to be caught. Temporarily.' Chance sipped his beer. 'If she told you anything different, she lied to you. You know I wasn't the first man in her life.'

'Y-yes,' admitted Rosalind reluctantly. 'She got heavily involved with men because she longed for security—for someone to love her and settle down with.'

'She picked the wrong man in me.'

'You married her.'

The sardonic expression slipped briefly to reveal a terrible fury. And then the lines of his face returned to their habitual mockery again. 'Not then, I didn't,' he said, a tightness still in his tone. 'And you can stop looking so disapproving. I was always quite open about my aims.'

'Yes,' agreed Rosalind bitterly. 'You wanted a good time.'

'Annie knew the score—as you all did. Dammit, Rosalind,' he said irritably. 'I'd played the dutiful heir for years, shut away in Paris studying, with tutors on my tail every time I looked like bucking the traces. I needed to enjoy myself. I didn't want commitment.'

'You didn't have to be so heartless! You soon dumped her and seduced *me*!' she blurted out reproachfully. 'You pretended to think about commitment then!'

His eyes flickered, glinting beneath the lowering lashes. 'You were different,' he said softly, his strong fingers investigating the logo on his glass. 'You played the subtle game and made me want what I couldn't have. That's why I stopped seeing Annie and was celibate for two months before I asked you out.' He smiled to himself and looked straight at her. 'I wanted to prove that I could exercise self-discipline when necessary. I wanted you so badly.'

She stared at him, hating him for his calculated tactics and for the fact that they'd worked. 'I thought you were serious about me,' she grated. 'Or I'd never have let you touch me.'

'Is that so?' he said in a non-committal tone.

She felt sick at his indifference to her feelings. They'd gone out together for some months and she'd fallen in love with him.

'You only pursued me because you couldn't bear to think a woman might not find you devastatingly attractive,' she said bitterly. The consequences of his love-making had changed her life. He had created an emptiness in her heart that nothing had ever been able to fill. 'You can't have been that enthusiastic,' she continued in a hard tone. 'You couldn't even get through your packing without making love to Josie!'

His smoky lids drooped over his glittering eyes and his lashes swept in a crescent over the prominent cheekbones. 'Quite a moment, wasn't it?' he said quietly.

Rosalind's breath caught sharply in her chest. 'I wanted to kill you!' she grated. The memory still had the power to hurt her. Chance, reaching out to Josie, who was standing naked among the folds of her dress... the terrible, searing accusations, his fury when she didn't believe his excuses... 'God, I despise you!' she whispered.

'But you don't despise Annie, despite the fact that she exceeded her role as my secretary in Martinique and, when we got there, promptly offered me sexual comfort,' he murmured.

'Which you accepted,' she said contemptuously. 'And Annie told it differently.'

'I'm sure she did,' he said harshly. 'And so she became the final winner of your girlish competition; she kept working for me and made herself indispensable; she was the one who stood by me when I needed someone. She——'

He frowned, checking himself. Rosalind furiously choked back her tears. Annie had presented Chance with a daughter. So he had married her. She blindly reached for her glass and almost knocked it over. 'Ohh!' She frowned in exasperation at her clumsiness.

'You're very edgy,' remarked Chance, lounging back and fixing her with a calculating stare.

'It's extremely unpleasant seeing you again,' she snapped.

'Regretting you ever left?' he murmured.

'Don't be insulting!' she fumed. 'Annie loves you——'

'Me? I doubt it. She was in love with marriage and all it brought. That is what she wanted—to be married—and I happened to be in her sights. By persisting when the rest of you fell by the wayside,' he said sardonically, 'she bagged all the prizes. Me, the Decatur emeralds and that coveted twenty-four-carat band on her finger.'

'Good grief, you're arrogant!' she gasped.

'Because I know that many women relentlessly pursue power and money?' he queried scathingly. 'At least I'm not fooled about my own worth. I came as a package, you see. I've never known whether women adore me, or what comes with me. That doesn't give a man much faith in the fair sex.' His mouth curled, increasing its sensuality. 'I own two plantations, I come from one of New Orleans's oldest families. I'm not physically unattractive, I enjoy spending money and I have my own teeth. Irresistible, eh? Who cares about looking for the man beneath, knowing if he bleeds, feels pain or sorrow, when you've got all that?'

She looked coldly at his jaundiced features. 'The alligator still appeals more.'

'There you go again,' he said silkily. 'You resist me, I try harder. It's that exciting, eternal chase of the hunter. Oh, come on, Rosalind! I know when word got around that Annie had failed to hold me that I'd be flooded with invitations. You've been a bit slow, but you're here, aren't you?'

'Don't flatter yourself,' she said calmly. 'That's not why I came.'

'I don't believe you. You're here because I'm a free man——'

'You always were a free man,' she said bitterly.

'And you were always a free woman,' he replied in a soft rasp. 'No man ever got to you, certainly not me.'

Rosalind marvelled that he could be so blind. And gained strength. She could fool him. 'Annie didn't tell me you were divorced,' she said quietly. 'I didn't even know you two were going through rocky patches——'

'Rocky! The damn boat's been rocking ever since I got in. I wonder why Annie's kept the divorce from you?' he said speculatively.

'Because she knew I'd come over like a shot and...'

Darn it! That sounded dreadful! She could have kicked herself. Chance was smiling in smug satisfaction. But she couldn't enlighten him as to the real reason why she was so anxious.

'Well,' he drawled. 'Don't you just *wish* you never said that?'

Her head lifted with proud disdain. 'I don't carry a torch for you and I don't have aspirations to being the second Mrs Decatur. You've always known that Annie and I are very close.'

'Are you? So close she never told you about the trauma of her divorce?'

'She would have realised I'd come over to New Orleans to comfort her,' she said coldly. 'I expect she didn't want me to take time off work.'

Haughtily she crossed her legs but the movement drew Chance's hypnotic eyes to them. Carefully she pulled down her skirt, which had ridden up to reveal the gleaming length of smoothly tanned thigh.

'Oh, the coy touch!' he mocked. 'I've seen further than that. I made love to you. I've stroked your entire body, inch by inch.'

A deep, burning anger energised her. How *dared* he throw that moment of mindless abandon back at her?

'I was an innocent fool,' she said coldly. 'It was certainly not an episode worth repeating. I'm no longer wet behind the ears and I have the sense to stay exclusive now.'

'You look exclusive. Being a man of taste, I'm tempted to buy.' His hand descended on her knee and pushed the skirt up again, the movement of the satin-lined material gliding over her legs and Chance's animal sexuality making every nerve lurch inside her. 'Expensive, are you?' he asked idly, his fingers warm on her thigh.

She suffered his touch with an air of stiffly offended dignity. 'Beyond price. Get your hand off my knee,' she said, rapping out her words like slow, lethal bullets.

He smiled unpleasantly and sardonically arranged her skirt in place again, every movement of his fingers a shafting torture. He chuckled triumphantly at her involuntary quiver.

'I don't buy your air of indifference,' he said huskily. 'Nor your explanation. If Annie really trusted you, she'd have wanted you to come.'

Rosalind coloured slightly, the colour deepening when she saw the gleam of mocking recognition of her discomfort in his eyes. 'OK. So I'm just as mystified as you why she didn't tell me. You bullied me into suggesting a reason before I could think it through.'

His eyebrow rocketed up in disbelief. 'Nice try,' he said condescendingly. 'But I'm tired of establishing reasons. Let's get on with the action. So, where are we doing this eating and wrassling? Your room?'

'The River View restaurant upstairs,' she answered, trying valiantly to remember that for the moment she needed to keep her temper—when she dearly wanted to slug him with her handbag.

He nodded. 'Upstairs, eh? All very convenient for your room afterwards—when you've wined and dined me and softened me up. Is that right?'

She stood up gracefully, discarding the impulse to hurl chairs at him. Her smile was charming and utterly false. 'Since patience is a virtue and anything remotely like a virtue is unknown to you, I can't expect you to exercise restraint. But do try to wait. I'd hate to spoil the surprise,' she said sarcastically.

Chance grinned like a cut-throat pirate and she felt her pulses jump around crazily. On the way to the forty-first floor, she gritted her teeth and shrugged away his arm, which had strayed possessively around her shoulders. She kept her eyes downcast, woodenly examining her dainty strap sandals, knowing he was taking stock of what she had to offer him physically, and she loathed every second she had to keep her anger in check and she loathed the way he was taking advantage of the situation.

When she found Annie and Melanie, she'd really plan a spectacular revenge.

They sat in the window, with the whole of the French Quarter and the sinuous sweep of the Mississippi River spread far below them. Rosalind looked out at the breathtaking view and felt an odd twinge of homesickness. She had loved this city as if it were her own. If things had turned out differently...

'Chance,' she said hastily, before she became maudlin. 'I need your co-operation.'

The hard, uncompromising eyes bored into her skull. 'I know you do,' he said smugly. 'Be nice to me and you might get it.'

Rosalind licked her lips nervously. She'd be lucky to get back to her room alone and in one piece. He didn't operate by rules. She'd seen enough of his working and womanising methods to know that.

'How nice?' she asked coldly.

'Sex will do fine.'

She put her shaking hands on her lap and clasped them tightly. What a vile opportunist he was. 'Not exactly the most subtle approach I've ever had,' she said huskily.

'You know the score. You want something, I want something.'

She glared at him with loathing. 'Do you often find it necessary to bully women into your bed?'

'Only the once, when I wanted a divorce,' he answered laconically.

'Chance!' she cried, shocked. 'Is that what happened?'

He opened his hands in a gesture of inevitability. 'Adultery? What else? She caught me with another woman.' He sounded offhand and Rosalind bristled with indignation on her friend's behalf.

'How could you?' she said unhappily.

'Oh, easy,' he snapped. 'You get another woman to take her clothes off and——'

'Stop it!' cried Rosalind, going white. 'I don't want to know the details.'

'You asked,' he said callously. 'Shall we have some champagne?'

They studied the menus and ordered their meal. Rosalind's eyes slid to Chance's hand, caressing the stem of his wine glass. That hand had touched her body with such intense sensuality and skill that she had abandoned all her principles. Her loins contracted and her eyes half closed at the deep pleasure that tortured her now with its delicious persistence. Oh, God! she groaned. The sensual attraction she'd thought long forgotten was still there, locked permanently in her deepest memories.

As if he knew, as if he could detect her intense feelings, his dark, enigmatic eyes met hers in a clash of mirrored desire. 'Bodies take longer than minds to learn sense, don't they?' he asked lazily.

Despite the cool air-conditioning in the restaurant, she felt the heat flooding through her, every part of her body alive to the aphrodisiac of his high-octane masculinity.

She craved the erotic touch of his demanding hands, his mouth. The air was positively humming with carnal lust and it wasn't just going one way, either; it was pulsing from her in waves.

She hoped he couldn't calculate blood-pressure at a table's distance. 'My only purpose in sticking this dinner out is to find out what has happened to my friend.'

'Then think on this. You need me,' he said softly. 'I'm your only link with Annie. Right?'

'Not quite.' She took a sip of mineral water to moisten her dry mouth. 'I can hang around the plantation and ask questions, I can go to the police, register her missing, and I can hire a private detective. You're not entirely my only hope.'

'Easier, though, to strike a deal with me,' he murmured, spooning up his clam chowder.

'A deal?' she frowned, a faint hope lifting her spirits.

'You make use of me, I...' He smiled mockingly. 'Oh, I am enjoying having you in my power. I intend to make use of you.'

Rosalind put down her fork, filled with a white-hot fury that left no room for food. She wanted to hit him. Her hands shook with the effort of not doing so.

All his life he'd treated women like casual playthings. Little kittens. The feminist movement would eat him alive. Male arrogance was bred into him and he'd taken to the old idea of *droit de seigneur* the way an alligator took to water.

'You are unbelievably self-centred! You may not be worried about your ex-wife and child, but I am,' she seethed. 'I'm upset and concerned and that's what's keeping me here—but make another crack like that and I'll sock you on the jaw with your wretched champagne bottle and try to get by without your help.'

'You seem to have done that already,' he said thoughtfully, eyeing her up and down and pricing everything as he went. His eyes glittered. 'Sugar daddy? Or oil?'

'Neither,' she answered irritably. 'I'm independent of men. I'm beyond their control, thank heavens.'

'Are you, now?' he said softly, a predatory look coming into his gleaming dark eyes. Rosalind wondered warily whether he meant to test that remark and felt a small shudder crawl up her spine. 'Nobody special in your life, then.'

'Tom. He's special,' she said quickly. Rosalind silently begged Tom's forgiveness. He was special—a wonderful boss—and he'd do as the lover Chance expected a sophisticated woman like her to have. She needed all the defences she could get.

'Are you working in New Orleans?' he asked idly.

'No.' With relief, she pushed the conversation into safer waters. 'I have a job in London,' she expanded. 'With Tom.'

'Cosy. London?' he repeated in surprise. He smiled at her, the picture of innocence. 'And what is that job?'

Rosalind reached for her glass and took a nervous gulp of wine. 'I'm a trouble-shooter. I'm hired to work for the kind of bosses other women won't,' she replied, wishing she were dealing with an overbearing ogre of a businessman now, instead of this maverick and unpredictable Frenchman.

He smiled faintly at the wary look in her eyes. 'Must have built up quite a thick skin,' he drawled.

'Thick enough to repel all who are unwelcome, yes.'

Beneath that confident, clear reply was a little voice of anguished pride. An urge rose within her to tell him how she'd cried for weeks after he had betrayed her, how he'd almost broken her spirit and how she'd fought her way back to make her own mark on the world with a vengeance. Then he'd know she wasn't to be trifled with. But caution kept her mouth clamped shut in a firm, hard line.

'And this . . . this tough career woman has come all the way from London to find a friend who hasn't written to her for a while?' he queried. 'Please,' he implored sardonically. 'Let's not strain my credulity too far.'

She fixed him with her clear blue eyes. 'I was afraid you might have thrown Annie and Melanie on the street.'

There was a breathless silence before he spoke. The veins stood out on his forehead and Rosalind was transfixed by the intensity of his anger poised beneath the sultry exterior. In the distance came the rumble of thunder, heralding the breaking of a New Orleans tropical storm. Rosalind nervously watched Chance's struggle with his own elemental nature.

'Would you like to explain that remark?' he asked in a tightly strained voice. 'Why you rate my ethics so low?'

Rosalind swallowed a couple of times and lifted her head bravely. 'You don't have any ethics. I know about Martinique,' she said huskily. 'Annie told me that you spent two years in prison for defrauding pensioners of land they'd bought from you.'

His eyes were cold and glittering with a dark fire. 'It was hushed up at enormous expense.' She took a deep breath. At the very moment she'd needed him, he'd been involved in a callous crime. His greed had cost her the most precious thing in her life. Chance's eyes flickered. 'It never occurred to you I might be innocent?'

'Hardly,' she said shakily. 'I already knew you were a con-man. And you were convicted.'

His mouth twisted. 'I was. It changed my life,' he said with a deeply felt bitterness.

She lifted her eyes slowly to his and caught her breath in fear at the anger she saw lurking in their depths. She forced herself to finish what she'd wanted to say since she had first began to worry about Melanie.

'I have to say it, Chance,' she whispered. 'I've spent the last few months afraid for Annie and Melanie, knowing how heartless you could be, wondering if you'd

grown tired of playing the father and husband and had
abandoned them...' She gulped, petrified by the way
Chance was looking at her.

'My God, Rosalind! If I ever had wanted to kill
someone,' he said harshly, 'it would be now.' He stood
up in a quick, angry movement, his eyes lacerating hers
with fury. 'I think you'd better come with me,' he said
through his teeth.

Rosalind stared up at him, incapable of moving,
cringing at the barely controlled violence that seemed
ready to erupt from his body when she didn't instantly
obey. And she wondered desperately what she should
do.

CHAPTER TWO

'I HAVE no intention of going anywhere with you at this moment,' Rosalind said coldly.

'I think you will, after a little token resistance,' Chance said in a low, savage snarl. 'I thought I'd got you out of my life. And then you zoom in on me like an irritating mosquito, searching for blood to suck.'

Rosalind fixed him with a baleful glare. 'I can assure you that my mouth won't come within yards of your flesh. My fist, maybe. A cut-throat razor, possibly. But it would make my skin crawl to touch you.'

'Something bothering you, Mr Decatur?' asked a worried waiter.

Chance flicked him a lethal glance and the man melted into the background hastily. 'If I prove to you that your fears are groundless and we find Annie and my daughter... What do I get out of it?' Chance asked baldly.

Her lips parted in astonishment. 'Melanie is your flesh and blood!' she said, aghast. 'Don't you have the remotest interest in knowing where she is?'

'Answer the question,' he hissed.

'You monster! You don't deserve her!' snapped Rosalind. Annie should never have let Chance see his child. It had been a mistake from the beginning. 'This is worse than I thought. You're not worthy of being a father!' she spat.

His hand shot across the table and enclosed her slender wrist. The thunder rolled through the air and huge splashes of tropical rain began to beat down on the windows. Light sheeted across the vast expanse of sky, making the other diners jump and exclaim, but Chance's eyes never wavered from hers for one second.

'I've already heard that in the divorce court,' he growled. 'Annie's lawyers made full capital out of my adultery.'

Rosalind flung up her head. 'Don't expect me to feel pity for you. You deserve everything you get,' she said vehemently.

'I don't want your pity. I want your body,' he said ruthlessly. His eyes lingered on her generous bosom, which was heaving in passionate emotion.

'Tough!' she snapped, disgusted by his bargaining. 'I don't want you, Chance. I'd fight every inch of the way if you tried anything.'

He smiled faintly. 'Alligator wrassling. What fun. All right. We'll settle for that.'

'We will not!' she insisted.

'Let's go and make a few phone calls from my office,' he said decisively.

She blinked, disconcerted. 'Phone calls? Your office?'

'Prefer your hotel room?' He smiled at her invitingly.

'Don't be ridiculous! But now? We——'

'Oh, I thought you were in one hell of a rush.' He thrust his hands in his pockets, watching her intently. 'Of course, if you want, we can munch our way through the hickory-grilled veal and bread pudding, have a few brandies——'

'You wretch! All right, your office, now,' she grated, angry that he was pulling the strings all the time and she was obediently jerking around like a mindless puppet. Though his office would be safe, with all those long-legged typists he liked to employ. She remembered what he'd said once—that he could hire efficient women, or efficient, beautiful women, and he knew which he pre-ferred to look at on a Monday morning.

'I'll get this.' He dropped a pile of notes on the table and took her elbow.

'I invited you to lunch——' she began haughtily, used to independence and objecting to this assumption that men paid the bills.

'I'm a southern gentleman,' he drawled. 'We don't expect our ladies to provide for us.' He grinned. 'Not in that way, that is.'

'Hey, Mr Decatur,' said the worried waiter. 'It wasn't that bad, was it?'

Chance chuckled. 'No, Sam. But it can't compete.' He leaned forwards confidentially. 'The little lady and I are in something of a hurry, you understand.'

How Rosalind got out of the restaurant she never knew. Perhaps anger drove her. She kept silent till they reached street level, but her frosty expression as she crossed to the revolving doors must have told him how she felt. If it didn't, he ought to have read the stiff lines of her body.

Torrential rain drummed a violent tattoo outside, sheeting down like a steamy Niagara Falls. The afternoon had turned nasty in more ways than one. The doorman sheltered them with his vast umbrella and she was obliged to cling tightly to Chance when they dashed to the waiting cab for the short trip to his office.

'Angry?' he asked in amusement.

'As a termite in a cooking-pot.'

He grinned. 'Hmm. It strikes me that you must have a pretty strong reason for keeping that beautiful mouth of yours shut, when you so obviously want to tell me what you think of me,' he observed, folding his long legs into the taxi. She couldn't bring herself to make any reply, but scowled at the wall of water outside, tense with the fear that her secret would be discovered. 'Hell. Do you hate me as much as I hate you?' he muttered.

She looked over and flinched at his hostile glare. 'Hate? I think I'm past that now I've seen you. Hatred would suggest strong emotions and you're beneath the effort,' she said huskily. 'I despise you for the shallow, vain, self-seeking man that you are.'

His jaw tightened imperceptibly. 'You need re-educating about one hell of a lot of things. I think I'm going to have to teach you a lesson,' he said menacingly.

'I won't be intimidated by you,' she gritted through her teeth. 'Particularly with that unoriginal remark.'

His hands shot out and roughly turned her face so that she was forced to look into the black pitch of his eyes, to be held like a 'gator fascinated by lamplight. Chance was just as dangerous as a ten-foot reptile, she thought, her limbs weakening. Given the opportunity, he'd drag her down to his lair and devour her inch by inch, enjoying every morsel of flesh.

'Don't be so clever. If you're not frightened of me, then you darn well ought to be,' he murmured, the heat of his breath making her skin prickle with awareness. 'I could break you. I could wipe that superior look of accusation out of your eyes and make you realise that everyone has flaws. Everyone is driven by emotions and responses which get out of hand if they're powerful enough.'

Passion motivated him, Rosalind thought shakily. It had once taken her over, and almost ruined her, and he knew nothing else. It was his weapon, his driving force and his flaw.

'Being hot-blooded is no excuse for your disgustingly promiscuous behaviour,' she said coldly, above the din of the drumming rain. 'Or your cold-blooded exploitation of those weaker than yourself.'

She clenched her fists tightly to stop herself from struggling with him. Only a cool head would help her to deal with Chance Decatur. She had no intention of losing her sanity twice over him.

'It's pointless arguing with you,' he said huskily. Lightning illuminated the sky with a blinding intensity and Rosalind's heart swooped at the sultriness of

Chance's mouth, the harsh carnality of his expression. He wanted her with a frightening need. He wanted to show he could still create turbulence in her life. 'You've no idea what passion is,' he growled. 'What you need is a thunderbolt to make you understand how helpless you can be in its grasp—and to force you to stop condemning people whose emotions are hotter than those of an iceberg. Dammit, it would be a service to society to melt you to that untouched core.'

He'd do it, she thought, her mouth dry. Just for a laugh.

'Are you getting out, mister, or are we here for the duration?' the cabbie yelled back at them.

Chance smiled unpleasantly, a kind of promising smile. The kind a sadist gave his victim just before inflicting pain. Unable to take any more of the tense atmosphere, Rosalind flung open the door and stumbled out into the hot rain, drenched in the few seconds it took her to run for the entrance to the massive, newly built glass and steel Decatur office block. Without waiting for him, she dived inside and stepped on to the long escalator.

He came up close behind her, his dark, raindrop-sprinkled lashes lowered lazily, and Rosalind folded her arms across her chest, knowing without looking that her saturated dress was enhancing her body a little too well.

'Don't even think it,' she warned, irritated by his laugh.

They swept through his suite of offices, shedding water as they stalked past astonished, envious rows of women who took out their resentment on their word-processors, the clacking of keyboards becoming noisier when Chance's hand strayed to Rosalind's neat bottom as it swayed along just in front of him, its form outlined provocatively in the straight, wet skirt.

She stopped, turned, and with cold deliberation she slapped his face, connecting with a satisfying sound, then continued on her way towards the president's office. His

lair, she thought nervously, acutely aware of the gasp of
shock which had run through the goggle-eyed women.
And of Chance's low chuckle.

'You will regret that,' he said in an undertone. 'More
than you know.'

She bristled, already regretting it, her fingers re-
taining the impression of the warm satin of his skin.
Rosalind clenched her teeth. What would he do to her?
she groaned to herself, upset that she'd awoken her own
senses when she'd sunk to his level of raw, unthinking
reaction.

'No interruptions,' he ordered to his dragon of a secretary. 'Not even for a tornado. I've got one of my own
here to handle.'

'Your appointment——' began his secretary.

'Postpone it.'

'But——'

He flung open the door to reveal a woman of
Rosalind's height and build, her fluffy hair bleached a
Monroe-blonde, her body swinging towards them
Monroe-style and with eyes only for Chance.

'Honey,' she cooed, all counterfeit fluttering lashes
and enormous overblown lips. 'At last—— Oh! Chance!
What *ever* you been doing? Y'all been in a *sauna*
together, or something?' she pouted.

'Blanche La Salle, meet Rosalind Baker,' murmured
Chance, looking rather delighted to see his unexpected
visitor.

'Hello. I'll leave you two together,' said Ros tightly.
He laughed wickedly, his teeth a flash of white in his
dark face. She recognised the sudden contraction of
Blanche's stomach. The woman ached for him. Inside,
Rosalind was seething, and it was a full five seconds
before she realised why. She was seething and…jealous,
she realised with a shock. She flushed with humiliation
that she should feel such an emotion about Chance.

'Honey,' began Blanche. 'I've been waiting——'

'First,' he interrupted, his eyes glittering, 'I'm not, by the remotest stretch of the imagination anyone's "honey". Second, I don't give a damn how long you've been waiting. Third, I have other things to do right now and you're going to get out of here and tell my secretary her job is on the line because she let you in.'

'Chance!' cried Ros, aghast at his ruthlessness.

'Darling, y'all *know* why I've come,' complained Blanche.

'Yes.' His eyes gleamed. 'But everyone in that office knows you were cited in my divorce. Let's have a bit of discretion, Blanche, shall we?' he murmured, flicking back the jet curls from his forehead in a shower of sparkling raindrops. 'If you're willing to do what I want, I'm delighted, but not now.' He slanted his eyes to Rosalind when she stiffened indignantly. His lips twitched and he turned back to Blanche. 'Let's keep this on ice. Out you go. I'll see you later. In private.'

'But——'

'Out!' he snapped. Blanche gave a sulky blink, glared at Rosalind and tried to leave with dignity.

'I hate the way you treat women! You're like a despotic emperor here, aren't you?' said Rosalind contemptuously. 'I suppose it's in your genes to treat people so high-handedly. A couple of hundred years ago you'd have made a perfect slave-master, forcing——'

'That's enough!' he ordered, a dangerous ring in his tone. 'Hallelujah! You women drive me mad! If you want to know about Annie, shut up and sit down!'

She did just that, shifting uncomfortably on the French *chaise-longue* in her wet clothes, shivering in the chilly air which made her skin feel clammy.

'Cold?' She nodded. Chance altered the room controls till she felt a blast of warmth. Then he went to an inner room, bringing out two fluffy white towels, throwing her one. 'There's a shower-room if you want to use it,' he offered gruffly. 'Warm yourself up.'

'No, thanks. You might walk in on me.' She flushed at the sultry softening of his face. He was thinking of the scene, of her water-slicked body, his gaze ranging hungrily over her. His lips parted and she hugged the towel around herself protectively, her own senses alarmingly aroused. 'And don't suggest I take my clothes off,' she said huskily. 'I'd rather keep them on and die of pneumonia.'

'What a waste that would be,' he said in a low murmur.

Rosalind unpinned her chignon and in silence they both towelled their hair, studiously ignoring one another. Then he picked up the phone and dialled a number, his broad back to her so that all her mind registered were the dark curls clustering damply on his dark neck, an expanse of shoulder and the lean hips. She lowered her gaze with a frown.

'Kate?' he growled, and Rosalind looked up with interest, recalling the family housekeeper, Cajun Kate, with a brief twinge of affection. Chance must have phoned a private number at the overseer's house where Kate lived. 'Where the hell is Annie?' He listened and heaved a sigh. 'What do you mean, she's not——?'

'I was right!' cried Rosalind in agitation. 'Oh, God!'

Chance covered the mouthpiece. 'Relax. She's taken a room in a hotel here, somewhere in town. Kate doesn't know where.'

Resenting the fact that it had taken him one quick call to establish what she'd been struggling to discover for endless months, Rosalind let out a slow sigh of relief. 'Thank God!' she said huskily.

He removed his hand from the receiver and spoke to Kate again. 'Why isn't she at home?' he barked. 'OK, OK. The shops are nearer. I get the picture——'

'Melanie! Ask about her!' interrupted Rosalind urgently, getting the drift of the conversation.

He gave her a baffled look. 'Who's looking after Melly? Right... No, I'm *not* coming back!' He slammed the phone down. 'You owe me an apology,' he said grimly. 'They're not living rough with a gang of hobos, bruised and battered in some dark alley, or holed up in the old slave quarters with chains around their legs or——'

'Oh, for heaven's sake! I'll apologise when I see them both, fit and well,' she snapped edgily. 'I still don't know where to look, do I?'

'Try any shopping centre,' he said coldly. 'Annie's blowing her alimony cheque on a wild shopping spree.'

'A six-month shopping spree?' she asked disbelievingly.

'Told you it was wild,' he drawled. 'No, Rosalind,' he continued, seeing her clenched fists. 'Save your passion for more worthy causes. She's only been in town the last two weeks. I was in touch with her before that. You're the one she's been avoiding for six months, not me.'

'What about Melanie?' she asked curtly.

'Probably dismantling New Orleans, piece by piece,' he said with a cynical curl to his mouth. 'I'm surprised we didn't hear the rumpus.'

Instantly alert, Rosalind sat up. 'What do you mean?'

'She's a brat,' said Chance heartlessly. 'A spoilt, ill-mannered, uncontrollable brat.'

'No!' she cried, appalled. 'I don't——' Realising he didn't know why she was so indignant, Rosalind stopped her intended outburst hastily. His words had upset her more than she dared to show. He was lying, of course. 'I don't believe you could say that about your own child.'

'Annie not tell you?' he mocked. 'My, oh, my, what a lot she's kept from you.'

'What do you mean?' she demanded.

'Melanie has a will of her own and it sure as hell doesn't fit in with the needs of society. The idea of obeying anyone is totally alien to her. She delights in bucking conventional niceties.'

'I'm sure you're exaggerating,' she said coldly.

'She's a little monster.'

'Takes after her father, does she?' snapped Rosalind.

'Oh, bitchy,' he drawled.

She lowered her eyes, ashamed. 'It was. I apologise. Though from your description I'd say she does sound like you. People never like seeing their own character traits in their children.'

'You'll learn the truth when you meet her,' he grunted. 'If anything, I've underplayed her bad faults.' He looked curiously at her white face and frowned. 'Are you all right?'

'Yes,' she lied. 'I'd like to use your phone, please. I think I'll ring a few stores to see if Annie's there.'

'Allow me.'

'Thank you.' Unhappily, Rosalind mulled over what he'd told her while he rang Jax Brewery and Canal Place. She didn't want Melanie to be a brat. Annie had given no hint that Melly was anything other than beautiful, clever, cute and adorable. She smiled wryly. Any mother wanted to think well of her child.

Yet because Annie hadn't told her about the divorce she was beginning to wonder what else had been kept from her. The thought was unnerving.

'They all remember Melanie,' Chance sighed, putting the phone down. 'Looks like Annie's heading towards the French Market. Try the Café du Monde. You might catch her there stuffing *beignets* into Melanie's mouth to stop her screaming.'

Rosalind winced at his unfatherly cynicism. 'You're a rat, making a joke about your daughter's behaviour!' she said accusingly. Poor kiddie, she thought sadly. She must have been exposed to some terrible rows in the process of the marriage break-up.

'What do you want?' he growled. 'Lies? Tears? Should I varnish over the truth? You don't imagine I *like* what she is, do you?'

'If Melanie is such a difficult child, shouldn't you shoulder some of the blame?' she asked bitterly. 'Divorce is unpleasant and bewildering for the innocent children caught up in it——'

'Do you think I don't know that?' he growled. 'That's why Annie and I only separated for a while. Why do you think I walked out, if not to save Melly from the sound of her parents arguing night and day?'

'If I know you, you walked out to live the life of a bachelor,' said Rosalind sharply. 'And what kind of father were you, not to guide Melanie better——?'

'I've had nothing to do with her upbringing,' he said harshly. 'Nothing at all.'

The shock made her falter for a moment and then she regained her composure. 'I bet! Too busy womanising!' she raged, beside herself with frustration. If only she'd been able to... She pushed down the thought and returned to the attack, her voice rising with suppressed misery. 'How could you be so irresponsible? You left Annie—who's always had a tendency to be over-sensitive——'

'Neurotic,' he corrected.

She glared and ignored him. '—to bring up your daughter because you had "better" things to do. It's unforgivable! You're responsible for——'

'Don't push me!' he warned savagely. He wrenched off his wet jacket and let it drop to the floor with the air of a man who knew a woman would come and pick it up. 'Go and find her,' he said through his teeth. 'Have your girls' reunion and keep well clear of me.'

She rose, increasingly alarmed about the unnerving facts she was uncovering and the terrible haunted look in Chance's eyes. 'Why has Annie not been in touch with me?' she asked apprehensively. 'It's deliberate, isn't it? What's going on? You have to tell me!'

His dark, secretive eyes flicked to her and away again as he angrily peeled off his shirt. Rosalind gulped. His body was harder, broader, more developed than before, and she stared at the gorgeous torso for longer than any woman between the age of fourteen and eighty should.

Her eyes were drawn to the planes and valleys of flesh and bone, the sheen of water highlighting the muscular definition. The perfect golden skin cried out for a woman's fingers and in her mind's eye Rosalind could see herself stepping forwards and sliding her palms up his body; she almost felt the touch of unyielding strength beneath her fingers.

Seconds ticked away, the electricity in the air higher between them than outside where the thunderstorm raged. Her body was throbbing and she couldn't move for dismay and desire.

'I'd forgotten,' he said softly, his voice loaded with the huskiness of lust. 'I'd forgotten what it was like to need a woman so badly that I'd trample over anyone and anything to get her.'

A pain shot fiercely through her heart. She gulped and tried to speak. 'Chance,' she managed in a croaky little voice. 'Leave me alone!' she whispered, as he slowly walked towards her.

Something rooted her to the spot. Something strong enough to stop her from running as she ought. For there was the same dangerous light in Chance Decatur's eyes that there had been the time he'd ruthlessly disregarded her half-delirious pleas and had taken her in broad daylight beside the Mississippi River. And her body ached to the core with the desperate urgency of that incredible moment and wanted to repeat it. Just once more.

'Remember,' he commanded softly. 'That day at Sans Souci—— '

'No,' she lied.

'You do. It was unforgettable. It's branded in letters of fire throughout my body. Every touch, every kiss, the scent of your skin, the texture of your hair when I lifted it so that it fanned out on to the grass above your head——'

She quivered and backed away, knocking a lamp to the floor with a crash that diverted neither of them, not even for a second. 'Stop this, Chance!'

'Why?' he enquired softly.

Disconcerted, she blinked. And found a reason, clutching at straws again. 'Tom. Don't you think you should consider him? Don't you have any respect for the fact I have a boyfriend?' she said in a hard, unnatural voice.

'I don't care if you have thousands,' he growled, his eyes glittering. He threw aside a heavy chair in his way as if it were matchwood and she jumped nervously. 'I don't care whom you date or what you are or why you're here. Only that I want you so badly that I'm not going to let you go. I'm going to make love to you. Hot and deep and passionate as we did a lifetime ago. And I'm going to do that right now.'

He stood still, rocking on his feet as if he could hardly move his limbs, and from him emanated a crushing sexual power that tempted Rosalind with an insane longing to throw caution to the winds and let him do just that.

The flames of need threatened to consume her totally. Chance had always broken rules, with the same casual ease that other men cracked crawfish, and women had always encouraged him. His aristocratic French background and the scandalous reputation he carried around so carelessly were dangerously, devastatingly attractive.

But there was too much pain inside her. The depression of those wasted years following his rejection washed through her in a purging flood and slowly wiped away all temptation.

He was the one who needed a lesson.

'Come to me,' he husked. 'Of your own free will. You owe me.'

Yes, she thought. She did owe him something, but not what he imagined ought to come his way. Suddenly Rosalind felt stronger than she ever had before. What did Chance know of passion, of true emotion? All he knew was a primitive, carnal urge. Diamond-hard inside, she proudly lifted her head.

She wanted to hurt him as he'd hurt her with a passion that rocked her through and through. He'd hurt her and been the cause of years of unhappiness. Now she had discovered that he'd emotionally damaged Melanie and hurt Annie with the sham marriage. Revenge might close the book on the Chance Decatur saga.

He'd kiss her and she'd remain indifferent and murder his pride. Her legs trembled and she squeezed the muscles tightly to keep herself upright and steady.

I hate him, she said to herself with every step. He ruined my life. Because of him I lost what I could have loved most. He left behind an empty shell of a woman, incapable of loving anyone because there was a gaping hole in her heart. It was as if he'd abandoned her in the middle of the Louisiana swamps and forced her to kick to the surface and survive.

Feeling quite dead inside, she lifted her face proudly. 'I want to catch Annie and get into some dry clothes,' she said flatly. He made no move to touch her. Kiss me! she urged silently. Give me the chance to spurn you!

'You're hunting for a better catch than Annie,' he said quietly.

'Not at all. I'm off alligator,' she answered, unable to resist the stab. Challenged by her, his head angled and came a little closer. Rosalind felt every ounce of her body begin to melt towards him and she knew she couldn't go through with this. So she stepped back and covered her confusion by impatiently checking the time by her watch. 'Oh! Is that the time? I really must fly——'

His eyes blazed at her casual attitude. 'Get the hell out of here!' he whispered savagely through clenched teeth. 'Before I——'

'More threats, Chance?' Inwardly shaking and loathing herself for taunting him—however successful she had been—she took out her compact and repaired the rain damage to her make-up. 'Sorry, I don't live around here and I'm neither impressed by your pedigree, nor do I fear any malicious backlash from you. And, despite your reputation for getting what you want, I'm sure even you don't dare to do anything rash, with all those tame females outside listening at the keyhole.'

Rosalind snapped shut the compact, stretched her newly bright lips into a charmless smile that didn't hit her eyes and turned on her heel. I won, she thought in stunned amazement. He didn't have the nerve to touch me because he thought I truly couldn't care less whether he kissed me or not.

But as she walked out, looking neither to right nor left, scrutinised in fine detail by the watching typists, she mourned with an inexpressible sadness the man she'd once fallen in love with. Not even the charm remained, nothing of that false overlay of urbanity and impeccably good manners. He seemed to have stripped away the civilised influences he'd learned in Paris to reveal the tough, unyielding core of the ruthless, primeval man beneath.

When she first set eyes on him, he'd just finished twelve years of being schooled and polished in France like his ancestors before him. In the past, *they* had set up mistresses, fathered bastards and finally married late in life to child-brides of impeccable purity and lineage. Chance had seemed intent on repeating the tradition.

She had been a challenge to him: sexually unaware, unwilling and highly moral. But he'd won her over slowly and inexorably, seducing her with such a subtlety that she'd never even noticed what he was doing. Of course,

once he'd made love to her, she'd ceased to fascinate
him.

Old story. Hurtful, nevertheless.

Rosalind took a deep breath, flung open the street
doors and stepped on to the glistening wet banquette,
the pavement steaming like a hazy curtain. Outside, as
well as in, the storm was over. The air was marginally
cooler now—perhaps only a mere eighty degrees—and
she realised her clothing was almost dry on her body.

The office was on the edge of the old eighteenth-
century French Quarter and she was within walking distance of the café in the market. Anxious to catch Annie,
she hurried through the narrow, shady streets, ducking
the drips from the plants decorating the pretty ironwork
balconies.

But, search as she might, she couldn't find Annie, not
that day or the next. And after a further few days of
checking hotel registers, wandering around the likely
spots in New Orleans and frequenting hotel bars, it
seemed she was making as much headway here as she
had in London.

Almost beside herself with worry, she walked up and
down Magazine and Royal, hoping beyond hope to see
Annie in one of the antique shops there. A silver limou-
sine cruised to a halt beside her, the smoked-glass window
slid down and with a sinking feeling she recognised the
driver. Chance.

'Found them?' he asked in a maliciously pleased voice.

Reluctantly she paused, her glance taking in the elegantly dressed Chance. Pearl-grey linen, cool panama
hat. Woman-killing gear. 'No. And I'll *throttle* you if
you've put them in danger by being indifferent to their
fates,' she rasped, and walked on blindly, feeling utterly
distraught and hysterical.

The car slid up to her again but she kept on going. 'I
believe I know where they are at this moment.'

She whirled around, her face joyful, the tears brimming up with the incredible relief. 'Oh, Chance!' she whispered shakily. 'Where? Where are they? Oh, dear God, are they both all right?'

Beneath the brim of his hat, his eyes were shadowy, but his mouth looked sour. 'Apart from nasty coughs from sleeping rough, yes,' he said, so sarcastically that Rosalind flushed at his mockery of her fears.

'Where are they?' she asked grimly.

'That kind of attitude's not going to win friends and influence people,' he drawled.

Her eyes blazed but she managed to modulate her voice. 'Please tell me where they are,' she said.

'Get in and I'll take you to them.' Yet still she hesitated, looking uncertainly at him. 'Hell, woman! This is not an abduction and I'm not intending to rape you on the front seat,' he snapped in exasperation. 'I have far too much respect for the upholstery.'

Rosalind bristled. 'I don't trust you. I'd rather go alone,' she said firmly.

'Then you'll miss her,' he said curtly. 'She's at Canal Place. Kate rang to tell me that Annie had returned to the plantation, collected some of her clothes and said she was going to Caché, to have them altered. But you'll have to hurry if you want to catch her there.'

She looked around for a taxi. Chance revved the engine as if he was going to drive away and she angrily ran to the passenger side and wrenched open the door, avoiding any glance at his smug face.

'I have no choice, do I?' she said ungraciously, slipping into the seat. 'You know I'm anxious to see if Melanie and Annie are OK.'

'Sure. You want to gossip about what a bad father and husband I was,' he growled.

Rosalind winced, her eyes searching his, then looked away, disturbed by the bleakness of his expression. 'You have a reputation for pleasing yourself and to hell with the rest of the world. You can hardly blame me for worrying,' she said quietly.

'I never treated you inconsiderately,' he said abruptly.

She held down a quiver. No. He had been gentle and thoughtful and tender when it had suited him. It had been a total sham. 'That doesn't mean anything,' she frowned, sitting forward in her seat, desperate to reach the shopping centre in time. 'I hope she's there,' she whispered, biting her lips as Chance accelerated through the narrow streets. Please let her be there, she added silently.

'You go on. I'll park the car.'

Needing no urging, she raced up the steps of Canal Place and took the escalator to the elegant, exclusive Caché salon where she and Annie had often paused, glueing their noses to the windows in rapturous envy. This time, she passed inside, to be greeted by a smiling, rather harassed assistant and the unmistakable sound of a child having a tantrum.

'I'm looking for Mrs Annie Decatur,' said Rosalind breathily, her eyes straying to the red-faced little fury thrashing around at the far end of the salon.

Melanie.

She stood stock-still. She'd been prepared for this moment but nevertheless her hand flew to her breast at the swoop of recognition and the sudden tightness in her chest. The joy of seeing her in the flesh at last brought a smile to her face. But the seven-year-old child was not the sweetly smiling little girl in the carefully posed pictures Annie had sent. This was a miniature tornado, angrily rushing through a rack of expensive ball gowns.

'Mrs Decatur is in the changing-room,' smiled the assistant with remarkable charm, considering the ear-splitting row coming from Melanie's small mouth.

The relief awakened Rosalind's limbs. 'Thank you!' she said huskily. 'I'll wait. Maybe I can reduce the decibels,' she added with a rueful and longing look at

Melanie. The child had Chance's colouring, his striking
air of arrogance. And his lungs.

'I want an ice-cream! Now!' yelled Melanie, squirming
grimly on the floor.

'If you shut up long enough, you might get one,' said
Rosalind drily, managing to stop herself from picking
Melanie up bodily and hugging her breathless.

Melanie was surprised and stopped beating her fists
in fury to look suspiciously at the woman standing above
her. 'Who the hell are you?' she asked rudely.

Rosalind hid a smile at the similarity between the child
and her father. It was just the kind of insolent remark
he'd make. Poor kiddie. No wonder she was difficult.
Look at the genes she had!

'I'm your godmother,' she said, the words long-
rehearsed and carrying no quiver of emotion.

'They have wands,' said Melanie sulkily.

'Stick around. I might use mine one day.'

Interested, Melanie sat up. Solemnly Rosalind held out
her hand to the child and the small, sticky fingers reached
out to take hers, almost dissolving Rosalind's composure entirely as she pulled Melanie to her feet.

'You're the one who sends me presents? From
England?' asked Melanie, her eyes rounding.

'That's me,' said Rosalind a little shakily.

'You write nice letters. I liked the funny-shaped balloons and the stars for my ceiling. But you could have
magicked them over here. You could have used your
wand.'

A warm smile touched Rosalind's soft lips. 'Perhaps
I'm saving it for a special occasion.'

'*Ros!*'

Thrilled and relieved to hear Annie's voice, she turned,
her arms outstretched in affection to see her friend in
her stockinged feet, thinner than she remembered and
dressed in a long-sleeved suit a size too large. She smiled,

glad that the dieting had worked. But Annie shrank back into the cubicle beyond, her green eyes big with alarm.

'Annie! It's me! What's the matter?'

'Why have you come?' moaned Annie, restlessly shifting from one leg to the other.

'You didn't write,' said Rosalind gently. 'I was worried.'

But Annie was looking over Rosalind's shoulder. 'Oh, God! Chance!' she whispered, the colour draining from her face.

Rosalind slowly twisted her head around and saw the panic-stricken Melanie scuttling away to paw her way into a rack of coming-out dresses, her sticky hands leaving marks on the virginal white material. Chance let out a bellow of anger and angrily strode towards Melanie. Quickly Rosalind put herself between the child and him, unhappy to see the fear he provoked.

'Melanie!' ordered Chance, glaring ferociously. 'Come out of there!'

'Shan't!' defied his daughter.

He swore under his breath. 'Do as you're told,' he growled in a manner that was not to be challenged. 'This instant!'

Melanie crept out and clung to Rosalind's legs, and she felt the trembling of the child's whole body. Picking her up protectively and sliding the slender little girl with motherly ease to her outflung hip, she glared at Chance. 'Why is she afraid of you?' she demanded heatedly. 'If you've ever laid a hand on this child's head——'

'Damn you, Rosalind!' Chance's huge chest inflated with barely suppressed fury. 'I seem to be a four-headed monster in your eyes!' he grated. 'She has a temper on her like a rhino. She's afraid of me because I'm the only one who insists on a bit of discipline—and gets it.'

'I hope you're telling the truth!' said Rosalind darkly, biting back what she wanted to say for Melanie's sake.

'She runs wild. She's as reckless as——'

'You,' she finished for him neatly. Her head went up at the dangerous flash of venom in his eyes.

'Go and apologise to the lady there for your thoughtless behaviour,' Chance commanded Melanie sternly, indicating the assistant. 'And ask her to send the cleaning bill to you. That's your allowance gone for this month... Annie?'

With Melanie sullenly obeying, he turned to Annie and a tingle went through Rosalind at the tremor that affected the nerves in Annie's gaunt face. She knew how Annie must feel, facing the man she loved: hurt, betrayed, despairing.

'W-w-what do you want?' stammered Annie. She drew her jacket more securely around her thin body, her hands and feet restless with nerves.

'To see if you and Rosalind welcomed each other with open arms,' he drawled. 'You didn't, so that story of yours about being friends is all hogwash,' he added, fixing Rosalind with glittering eyes. 'My suspicions were warranted.'

'Annie was startled,' said Rosalind confidently. Happy at last, she smiled gently at her old friend. 'It's wonderful to see you,' she said, walking towards her. She reached out for a long-overdue embrace.

'Don't!' said Annie quickly, wrapping her arms around herself. 'I don't like being touched!'

Rosalind saw how Annie had backed into the corner, her eyes standing out above pale, hollow cheeks. 'What is it?' she asked quietly. Annie flushed a bright scarlet and slanted her eyes at the ominous-looking Chance. 'Why are you so afraid of him?'

'He makes Mommy cry!' complained Melanie. She ran to her father and kicked him in the shins, his flinch more a question of wounded pride, Rosalind thought, than pain.

But the dark face was implacable when it turned back to the two women in the cubicle. 'She's seeking attention,' he said quietly, his hand closing around Melanie's.

'Then give it to her!' cried Rosalind passionately. 'In the form of love! Can't you see that's what your daughter needs?'

His eyes flickered with a strange, chilly light. 'The devil take you,' he whispered bleakly.

'Not without a fight,' she countered and studiously turned her back on him. 'Annie,' she said softly. 'I'm here because I was going frantic wondering about you two.'

'Melanie can take care of herself. I'm the one who needs to be looked after,' said Annie resentfully.

Rosalind stared. Patiently she continued, her worries increasing by the second because something was very wrong. 'I would have come if you'd asked. But you didn't return my calls. If you're in need of a friend——'

'I need more than that,' mumbled Annie self-pityingly, shivering despite the warmth of her spring-weight suit.

Rosalind thought she looked ill and her face grew anxious. 'Then lean on me,' she said with loving warmth. 'If Melanie is a handful, I can help——'

'I wish you would!' cried Annie fervently. She kept her eyes averted from Rosalind, as if unwilling to make contact. 'She's so demanding. She's had three *beignets* this morning already. Nothing but eat, eat, eat...'

'Children have enormous appetites, Annie,' Rosalind said, puzzled. 'Don't you remember seeing that kiddie on the steamboat cruise, spending the whole trip eating roast beef and gravy po-boys?' She smiled, recalling how she'd been awed by the way the lad had stuffed the great chunks of the French bread into his small mouth.

Annie shuddered as if the thought was physically painful to her. 'Come to Sans Souci,' she pleaded. 'Stay for a while. You can supervise Melanie's meals. You can do something about her table manners. Please, Ros; you

were always so calm and level-headed. I need that kind
of person around me.'

'And,' said Chance curtly, 'I think Rosalind deserves
some explanations. So, for that matter, do I. You look
terrible, Annie.'

'That's not very kind,' winced Annie.

'Someone has to tell you,' he said callously. 'I'll drive
you all to the plantation. You can give me supper——'

'*No!*' cried Annie hoarsely, her expression one of
loathing.

'Mommy always eats alone,' announced Melanie. 'In
the hotel, Mommy has room service. She eats when I'm
asleep.'

'And who do you eat with, Melanie?' frowned Chance.

'Me. Me and the telly.'

'No wonder you don't know how to eat properly!'
Chance glared. 'Last time I took you out, you were a
disgrace!'

Rosalind frowned. The hang-up about food reminded
her of something...someone... Her brow furrowed and
she looked at Annie's constantly restless body
thoughtfully.

'Like it or not,' snapped Chance, breaking into
Rosalind's thoughts, 'we're having supper together. You
can explain for a start why you don't like living at Sans
Souci.'

'No——' began Annie.

'Refuse and you don't get your alimony this month.'

Both Rosalind and Annie winced at his blatant attempt at blackmail. 'Stop bullying your ex-wife! Any
settlement you made on Annie isn't negotiable on your
casual whim, it's hers, by law,' said Rosalind grimly.

'I acknowledge one law,' he snapped. 'Possession.'

Melanie began to tap-dance in the entrance to the salon
and before Chance could think about objecting to the
noise Rosalind touched Annie's arm confidentially. 'It's
OK, let me deal with it,' she murmured. 'Melanie!' she

called. 'Come and tell me which earrings suit me best, would you? I need some female input on this.' She muttered in Annie's ear. 'We can handle Chance,' she said. 'Don't let him bother you. Finish dressing. Let him drive us to the plantation if he wants. What do we care?'

Annie seemed glad to leave everything to Rosalind, and disappeared into the cubicle. Melanie flounced over suddenly, keeping a wary eye on the brooding Chance. 'We don't want him,' she announced loudly. 'He'll only set Mommy crying again.'

Steadying her shaking hands on the glass counter, Rosalind blindly reached out and hastily fixed what looked like a pair of chandeliers to her lobes, upset at Melanie's revelations. Chance made every woman he encountered cry, one way or another.

'What do you think?' she asked brightly.

'Bit Christmas-treeish,' said Melanie honestly.

In the mirror, she saw Chance's reluctant smile—proud, quirking his mouth into that appealing, disarming lop-sided grin which had charmed half the women in New Orleans and the length and breadth of River Road all the way to Baton Rouge. Despite what he said, she knew he did love the child—so why did he pretend he didn't? Was it his remorseless pride, because Annie and Melanie had rejected him? A stupid male cover-up to protect his self-esteem?

Her fingers fumbled with the next pair of earrings and he stepped forwards, taking them from her and turning her around to slip them on with the expertise of a man who had repeatedly clipped thousands of dollars' worth of valuable jewellery to the ears of captivated women, his hands warm, sending quivers of electricity sparking down her body.

'Beautiful,' he breathed. 'Don't you think so, Melly?' He lifted the child up and she wriggled in his grasp, but with the inconsistency of childhood she was immediately diverted by the jet and diamond earrings, her little

fingers gently persuading the dangling cascades of jewels
to swing backwards and forwards.

Rosalind's eyes filled with emotion at Melanie's parted
lips and rapt expression. She might be a brat, but the
right guidance would turn her into a child any mother
would be proud of. She gulped back the words she longed
to say.

'She'll take them. Put them on my account,' said
Chance casually to the assistant, putting Melanie down.

'No!' said Rosalind quickly, not wanting anything
from him.

'Take the damn things. You can do something for me
in exchange,' he said in a soft undertone. 'Take a look
at Annie. Talk to her. Something's wrong and she won't
let me near enough to find out. She's lost a lot of weight.
I want to know if she needs specialist treatment. Some
disease, maybe...' His voice trailed away.

Rosalind stared back at him with solemn eyes. He
sounded very concerned and that touched her. 'Losing
weight? Oh, Chance, are you thinking of cancer?'

'Could be.'

She saw the lines of anxiety creasing his face and the
flare of pain in his eyes. 'Chance! You—you *care* for
Annie?' she faltered, absently accepting the boxed
package from the assistant. 'Thanks,' she said, on auto-
pilot.

'You're welcome, ma'am.'

'Ros——' he began.

His jaw clenched and she knew it was to keep back
emotion. Her mind whirled, going through the copious
descriptions Annie had sent her of their ardent courtship
in Martinique, before he was flung in prison. Chance
had been in love with Annie then. Judging by his vulnerable expression, Chance loved Annie even now. This
marriage could be saved, for the sake of Melanie, as well
as the parted lovers.

'Oh, Chance,' she said sadly. 'If we could wipe out the mistakes of the past, the foolish, thoughtless errors——' She couldn't go on. He was looking at her with such yearning that it wrenched her heart in two. Her eyes sparkled through misty tears. Melanie's future wasn't in pieces after all.

'If only we could,' he husked.

'I hoped you felt that way,' she said softly.

'I do,' he muttered. 'We must get back together. Nothing less will do.'

The pain of envy, for a love as searing as Chance's for Annie, reached down inside her, as destructive of all her sensitive nerves as if he'd ripped her open. 'Chance,' she said in a choky little voice, 'of course I'll come to the plantation for supper—and I'll talk to Annie. Leave it all to me. Everything will be all right.'

Unconsciously, she had hugged the child to her and Melanie's arms had gone trustingly around her neck. Full of heartache, she wanted to cry.

Oh, it was such a long, long time since she had held her own child in her arms.

CHAPTER THREE

ROSALIND could hardly bear it. Melanie was her own flesh and blood but didn't know. And yet when she snuggled into little Melanie's soft face she sensed an instinctive bond between them.

'Do that again!' Melanie laughed with pleasure.

Chance looked back over his shoulder, his dark eyes softening to the consistency of molasses when Rosalind laughed adoringly and nuzzled her daughter once more, a sigh of contentment on her lips as they left the building together.

'You're all cuddly,' declared Melanie dreamily. 'Sort of soft and cushiony.'

Chance gave a low chuckle and Rosalind blushed, aware that he could see that Melanie's slender body was pressed firmly against Rosalind's voluptuous breasts. The rake-thin Annie shot Rosalind a nervous look and Rosalind sought to reassure her friend.

'It'll be OK, Annie,' she said gently. 'Don't begrudge me these few moments.' She smiled warmly and Annie responded with a quivering little grin.

'Sit in the front, Rosalind,' ordered Chance, when she made to sit in the back next to Annie. 'I'm not a chauffeur.'

'I want Rosalind here!' shouted Melanie.

'And I want her *here* and I'm bigger and meaner than you,' said Chance grimly, his eyes clashing with his daughter's in the driving-mirror.

'If it's of interest to anyone what *I* think, I'd like to see the scenery. It's been a long time since I made this drive,' said Rosalind, trying to be diplomatic. She slipped into the passenger-seat with a sigh. Chance didn't make things easy. But then he never had.

'You've been here before?' asked Melanie. 'Like...when I was little?'

'No,' said Rosalind shortly. 'Before then.'

'So y'all was Daddy's friend as well as Mommy's?'

She gave a small grimace which she didn't let Melanie see. 'Yes, of course,' she said brightly. 'We were all friends——'

'Yeah, Josie too, I know,' said Melanie. 'Mommy says Daddy and Josie were like *that*.' She waggled her tightly linked forefinger and middle finger in Rosalind's face.

Her troubled eyes sought Chance's reaction. His jaw had tightened a little, but that was all, and when he looked at her his expression seemed amused and rueful, as if he regretted his liaison.

'What happened to Josie?' she asked quietly.

'I sacked her,' muttered Chance.

'Because I walked in on you both?' whispered Rosalind, annoyed at his twisted logic.

'Because she was a conniving, scheming little minx,' he growled. 'It's in the past. She married a senator. Don't feel sorry for her. We must forget it. Start anew,' he said quietly and Rosalind nodded, her face bright with hope.

'Why did you leave England?' demanded Melanie. 'I wouldn't leave my home for *anything*, nor my pony. I'll show you him.'

'Thanks,' said Rosalind warmly, aware of the honour. It gave her a strangely pleasant feeling to tell her daughter something about herself. 'Your mommy and I grew up in the same street in London together.' In the circumstances, she decided to omit the part about their unhappy home lives. She'd tell Melanie when she was more settled. 'We were teenagers, just out of secretarial college, and we came to America in search of adventure.'

'Did you find any?'

'More than she could cope with,' murmured Chance.

Surprisingly, she found herself exchanging a wry smile with him. Adventure had come in the form of the young French Creole, Chance Broussard Decatur, with his exciting mix of French and Spanish aristocracy. It had come in the Vieux Carré, the French Quarter of New Orleans, with its sound of impromptu jazz filling the streets, the chatter of many languages on the lacy ironwork balconies and in its flower-filled Spanish patios.

'Is he right?' demanded Melanie.

'In New Orleans? Are you kidding?' grinned Rosalind.

'Why leave, then?'

Rosalind hesitated, highly conscious that Chance's body had tensed. 'Oh, your daddy and mommy went to work in Martinique, and I just thought I'd go home,' she said casually.

'It's real neat that you're all together again,' said Melanie enthusiastically.

'Real neat,' said Chance drily, and grinned broadly at Rosalind.

She felt her heart lurch uncontrollably and turned to stare blindly out of the window. Dear heaven, had she no man-sense at all? No wonder she'd succumbed to his persistent demands all those years ago if she still found him attractive despite everything she knew about him, despite the fact that he was bound soul by soul to her best friend.

'Like some music?' murmured Chance, breaking in on her memories. She shrugged her indifference and then wished she'd chosen. ' "Moon River",' he said huskily. 'I played it the first time I drove you to the plantation. We'd been dating two months and two days.'

'Really?' she said, pretending not to remember. Two months, two days and twelve hours, she thought to herself. And she'd been thrilled that he was taking her to the plantation, Sans Souci—Without Care. She'd been without a care in the world then and life had been sweet, with Chance's kisses the highlight of her days and the conviction that he loved her and no other woman.

He'd told her he was going to Martinique at short notice and she'd been miserable that he wouldn't take her. They'd be parted for weeks.

'We have to say goodbye,' he'd murmured. 'Say goodbye to me so I remember it.'

She had drawn in a sobbing breath and, without speaking again, he had driven to a secluded place by the river and laid siege to her vulnerable heart, seducing her so cleverly that she'd believed she had willed it to happen. The ferocity of their desperate hunger had haunted her dreams for years, making her break into a cold sweat at her shameless lack of inhibition.

He'd touched her deepest emotions. She'd lain in his arms, utterly content that he loved her, cradled in false security.

When she'd drifted in during the small hours of the morning, Josie had laughed at the idea that Chance was contemplating marriage.

'You fool!' Josie had said scathingly. 'At least he's got enough sense not to get you pregnant.'

Her face had flamed a bright scarlet. Chance had been careful. In her innocence, she did not know then that nothing could ever be totally safe. 'He loves me,' she'd muttered in defence of her behaviour.

'God, you're gullible, Ros!' Josie had hissed. 'He tells us all that! He couldn't get you any other way, could he? Darn it, he'd go with any woman who looks good and is willing!'

'You won't talk about him like that!' seethed Rosalind. 'He's been faithful to me——'

'Chance Decatur, faithful?' Josie gave her a pitying look. 'I'll prove he's lying, for your own good.'

'How?' she asked angrily.

'You'll see. You'll believe the evidence of your own eyes.'

And she had. But the pain she'd felt on seeing Chance reaching out so eagerly for the naked Josie had paled in comparison to the agony of surrendering her child to him.

Rosalind's face went very white. Chance thought Annie was Melanie's mother. And that was how it had to stay. It was no good being upset now. Annie had been doing her a favour by fostering Melanie. It had been an awful twist of fate that he'd assumed Melanie was his child and Annie's when he came out of prison. Her mouth drooped unhappily. If a woman met you with a child in her arms who looked just like you, it would be the natural conclusion to come to.

She only wished she'd been well enough to have known what was going on. Her postnatal depression had lasted for more than six months. If she'd been more aware, she would have fought for her child and not gone along with Annie's suggestion that she didn't enlighten Chance. Annie was convinced that Melanie would be better off living with him. Instead, Rosalind thought miserably, her daughter had been subjected to a broken marriage caused by a philandering father.

'Dollar for your thoughts?'

She turned stormy, anguished eyes to Chance. 'They're not worth a cent,' she whispered, her mind in turmoil.

'Ros...' His hand reached out to touch her thigh but she forestalled it, knocking it away, upset that he had the gall to touch her when his family were in the back of the car.

'I saw that! Don't you hurt my godmother!' said Melanie belligerently from the back seat. 'She'll bash you with her wand.'

Chance winced. 'I'm your father. Speak respectful, do you hear?'

'Earn that respect and she might,' muttered Rosalind in an undertone, for his ears only. She turned and smiled at Melanie, who was bouncing up and down beside the tense Annie. 'We both went for the same mosquito,' she lied guiltily.

'Quick thinking,' admired Chance.

'I'm boosting your father-image,' she muttered.

'Don't waste your time. Annie's ruined that,' he said bleakly.

Rosalind's tender heart ached. These three people were all on edge with each other and they needn't be, shouldn't be. They all needed love and to trust one another, to feel free to show their affection freely again. She yearned to enclose them all in her embrace.

'It's not too late,' whispered Rosalind anxiously.

'I've got a star on my bedroom door,' said Melanie importantly.

'As well as the ones on your ceiling? I'd like to see that,' smiled Rosalind with a rush of warm feeling at her daughter's pride. 'It won't take long before I can, will it?' she added, checking the passing scenery.

Already they were past the suburbs and into Cajun country, thick with swamp cypress trees and their hanging draperies of grey Spanish moss. The wilderness crowded in on the highway threateningly. The swamp waters, level with the road and glinting in the late afternoon sun, gave a hint of the complicated maze of slowly moving bayous, the creeks beyond.

'Are y'all stayin'?' asked Melanie in a small, hopeful voice.

'Are *you staying*,' corrected Chance. 'Where do you learn to talk like that?'

'Cajun Kate,' said Melanie casually. 'An' Blanche. I spend as much time with Blanche as you, Daddy.'

Rosalind gasped and flashed a disapproving glance at Chance. His jaw tightened and his dark eyes swept up to the driving-mirror, treating his daughter to a baleful glare.

'But I'm not learning bad things off her as a result,' he muttered. 'What the hell do you do all day, Annie?' he frowned. 'I don't want Melanie talking casually and growing up like Blanche.'

With some difficulty, Rosalind bit back the temptation to say that Blanche suited *him* well enough and it was probably a matter of opinion who was learning bad things.

'Don't pick on me!' sighed Annie. 'I do the best I can.'

'I could stay,' Rosalind said to Melanie, diffusing the tense atmosphere with her enthusiasm. 'For a short while. If your mommy and daddy say that's OK.'

Satisfied, the little girl lolled against Annie, who pushed her away irritably. Rosalind pretended not to notice, but she felt upset. Didn't Annie love Melly? All these years, the stories she'd told about their picnics together, the visits to the zoo...

'You're doing a lot of thinking,' said Chance softly.

She smiled wistfully and cast around for a reason. 'It's seeing Louisiana again,' she said huskily.

Given half a chance, she mused, the swamp would take over the highway, River Road and uptown New Orleans in just two or three years, reducing the trappings of civilisation to untamed land again. They were very close to the anarchy of nature here. Her mouth curved in amusement. Too close. Southern passions tended to be a mite too uninhibited for well-brought-up English girls.

'Miss it?' he asked lightly.

'To be honest, I've missed it all more than I thought,' she admitted. 'I've missed the openness and friendliness of the people in New Orleans. I like the fact that they love talking to strangers and make them feel welcome,' she smiled. Her eyes followed a group of egrets as they

rose from the almost submerged knuckle-like roots of a
cypress tree, lifted their wings and soared into the deep
blue sky. 'And out here it's raw and wild. A little frightening, but exciting, as if we're on the edge of danger.'

'Everywhere is wild beneath the veneer of civilisation,
Rosalind,' Chance said quietly. 'Don't be fooled.
Wherever you are there's danger. We're all savages in
certain circumstances.'

She took that as a warning and a promise, a little un-
settled by his statement. He thought it normal to be
savage. 'I don't think so,' she said stiffly.

'If there aren't people or causes you'd die for, then
you're only half alive,' he said fervently.

Her brow furrowed. He was right. She'd fight tooth
and nail for her daughter. She could be a savage, too,
if necessary. Chance turned off down Decatur Road and
Rosalind's heart ached to see the centuries-old oaks
again, arching over them in a living tunnel, eighty feet
wide. She and Chance had strolled here, hand in hand
in the shade, planning their future.

'It looks smarter now, more cared for,' she said, con-
tinuing her train of thought, noticing how neat the grass
edges were, and that the azaleas and hydrangeas were
lusher than before.

'My parents had neglected it when I took it over,' he
answered curtly. 'I lavished time and care on the house
and grounds when I came back from Martinique.'

Rosalind remembered that his globe-trotting parents
had left him in boarding-school and he'd said they'd
hardly ever been around when he'd needed anyone.

'If they hadn't died in that fire in Manila, would you
ever have left Paris?' she asked curiously.

'No—and I would have missed living here, wouldn't
I?' he said, looking around with pleasure as if he longed
to be back permanently. Rosalind smiled, thinking it
would be easy to get Annie and Chance back together.
'I suppose I would have put down roots in France.'

Chance's hand rested on her knee and she went rigid. 'I think you should put down roots here again,' he said in a sultry whisper.

Now, even now, she thought miserably, he had the power to arouse her. *Then*, she'd had the excuse of innocence and of being driven by the sweet despair of the imminent parting. What reason could she plead now to explain her reaction to him? The romantic music drifted into Rosalind's subconscious mind, tormenting her.

'Chance,' she said urgently, not wanting to be heard in the back, 'don't throw away this opportunity you have to heal old wounds. You don't have to prove your virility to me——'

'No,' he husked. 'I don't, do I? You have evidence of that.'

She winced with the painful breath that sliced through her defenceless body. He couldn't mean Melanie! He must have been referring to his torrid lovemaking. She went pink and willed away the scurry of arousal that was feeding her hungry body.

'This is not the time or the place,' she said in an undertone.

'OK. Later, then,' he said, amused.

'Why are you two whispering?' demanded her daughter. 'Secrets is rude.'

'Are rude,' corrected Chance, frowning. 'And I told you before about being cheeky.'

'And precocious. You usually add that. You forgot the precocious this time,' Melanie pointed out in delight.

He stopped the car and flicked off the security locks. 'I'm not in the mood for smart back-chat. Out. You can walk.'

'It's dark in them thar trees,' said Melanie suddenly.

Rosalind tried not to giggle at the dramatic tone of voice. 'It's a lovely idea!' she cried with enthusiasm, relieved to have an excuse to escape the oppressive atmosphere and Chance's wandering hands. 'Well done,

Chance. Come on, Annie, we'll have a girls' gossip on the way.'

Melanie leapt out with an excited squeal and, pleased, Rosalind reached back and caught hold of Annie's arm eagerly, then felt shock run through her body. Beneath the concealing cloth it seemed that her friend was nothing but a living skeleton.

'Annie!' she whispered.

Annie wrenched open the car door and stumbled out, leaving Rosalind in stunned silence. She sat in dismay, watching Annie's undignified progress along the oak alley, her painfully thin wrist evident as she grimly dragged along the yelling Melanie.

'What is it?' asked Chance hoarsely. He took Rosalind's hands in his and she saw from his expression how anxious he was about his ex-wife. 'For God's sake, Ros, tell me what's upset you!'

She licked dry lips. 'I'm not sure...'

'Oh, Ros. I am,' he whispered, turning her hands over and kissing her palms.

The heat of his mouth scalded her flesh and she snatched her hands away, staring at him with horrified eyes. 'Why do you keep *touching* me?' she moaned, bewildered.

'Because I have to,' he muttered, smoothing out the lines in her brow with gentle fingers. His gaze drifted speculatively to her parted lips.

'No,' she mumbled.

'I want you,' he breathed, his voice throbbing.

Her whole being surged with a longing that knocked all sense out of her head. Wildly, she considered telling him to go ahead, to kiss her, make love to her, take what he wanted until his appetite was appeased. And hers. For a crazy moment it seemed the only answer to this continuous torment, because once he was over this compulsion to dominate her it would then leave him free to consider his relationship with Annie. A peacock screamed, bringing her to her senses.

'Oh, dear heaven! Annie!' she cried in remorse. 'Oh, Chance! I think I know what and why she's been hiding from you! I think she's anorexic!'

'What?' He started, then twisted around and it seemed he looked at Annie's distant figure as if for the first time. 'Anorexic? She's thin,' he conceded. 'But so are many fashionable women. They've forgotten how women should look,' he added sourly. His glance lingered on Rosalind's unquestionably female body. 'Why do you think it's anorexia and not just pure skinny? She's been watching her waistline for years. Don't all women?'

'Not to that extent. I certainly don't. Chance, I was in a clinic once,' she said quietly. 'For severe clinical depression.'

Caused by you and the birth of your child, she wanted to add. But this wasn't the time. One day she'd face him with the consequences of his heartlessness—— No, not all of those consequences. The secret she nursed about Melanie must stay just that, a secret between herself and Annie.

He was looking at her strangely. 'You, depression?'

'Don't ask,' she said grimly. 'I'm not prepared to talk about it. I met a lot of anorexic women at the clinic and I recognise some typical signs: thin, of course, wearing baggy clothes to hide the weight loss, feeling the cold—and she was having a load of clothes altered at Caché.'

He was giving her his whole attention now. 'Go on,' he said, the deep crease slicing between his dark brows. 'What about eating in private?'

'She'd want to conceal the fact that she's denying herself food. And it is a denial—she wants to eat as much as anyone. The sight of food would torment her. Oh, and she's terribly restless. I knew a girl at the clinic who'd spend the whole day running on the spot to consume calories. It was awful, hearing her above me, knowing her desperation.'

'It sounds hell,' he said sympathetically.

'It was hell,' she answered tightly. 'For me as well as the girl.' You drove me there. No one ever knew the agony I went through.

'Anything else?' he asked huskily.

'Well——' She bit her lip and went silent.

'Well, what?' asked Chance grimly, his eyes dark secrets.

'There's usually a reason why anorexics try to withdraw from responsibility——'

'She doesn't have any responsibilities,' he growled. 'I shoulder those.'

'But she has Melanie,' said Rosalind quietly, her heart thudding. Annie had shown little interest in her fostered daughter... almost a resentment... Had Annie felt so guilty at deceiving Chance that it had preyed on her mind? 'It's clear that she doesn't spend time with Melanie. And she wanted me to help look after her,' she explained.

'Hell, you can't mean she wants to abandon her to a virtual stranger?' He looked at her coldly. 'No mother seriously contemplates giving up her child! What kind of a heartless bitch of a woman would ever do that, Rosalind?'

Knives twisted in her body and she gave a little moan, her eyes huge, mesmerised by his. If he ever knew... 'A—a sick and desperate woman,' she whispered, speaking for herself, as well as Annie.

'You sound very upset,' he frowned. 'You care deeply for the people you love, don't you, Rosalind?'

'Yes. I do,' she mumbled.

He took her shoulders gently and she wanted to let him hold her. She needed to cry. 'I'm glad,' he said simply.

His warm, admiring smile went straight to her heart and Rosalind struggled to keep her thoughts on Annie. 'Chance, Annie's own problems are enough to bear without coping with a difficult child. Don't be hard on her,' she pleaded. 'Remember her as she was when you married her, not as you see her now. You might think she's self-centred—well, she probably hates herself. She's not acting rationally...' Her voice petered out. He wasn't listening but seemed to be staring at the two figures far ahead, barely breathing at all.

'Self-hatred,' he muttered. His bitter mouth shaped a silent but identifiable expletive and the force of his feeling tempered her shock at the curse.

'Don't blame yourself totally,' said Rosalind softly.

'What?' His head jerked around as if he'd woken from a deep sleep, confusion and heart-aching vulnerability still written on his face. And then he ruthlessly eliminated them. 'I see no reason to blame myself,' he said harshly. 'Annie's had everything she wanted——'

'But the divorce—finding you and Blanche together——'

'Any number of events could have made an impact on Annie's ego,' he muttered. 'Most of them you seem in ignorance of. We must get help for her.'

'She has to want help first. If it is anorexia, then she'll need counselling and some time in a clinic to be treated,' she said, determined to get the point through to him and not be diverted by his bad grace. 'The regime is no easy ride.'

'That could be awkward. How long a while?'

'Months.'

He heaved an exasperated sigh. 'What a mess. And Melanie? What happens to her?'

'You must take on that responsibility, of course!' she exclaimed in surprise. 'You must stay with her, here at the plantation——'

'Only if you do.'

Rosalind gave him a sharp warning look. 'Now, Chance——'

'That's my decision,' he said, driving on. 'Take it or leave it.'

'Don't be ridiculous!' she said irritably.

His profile remained obdurate.

For a few moments, however, she was distracted. The oaks, with their understorey of camellias, opened to unfold the manicured gardens in front of the Decatur mansion, a pure *Gone With The Wind* plantation home, built in the nineteenth century when the Mississippi was the main highway, when cotton was king and the plantation owners were the wealthiest people in the whole of America.

Sans Souci lay serene among its skirts of banana trees and crape myrtle, rising like a fancy cake iced in a delicate soft blue, decorated with white-painted Grecian columns and a massive double cypress-wood staircase leading to the wide, shady gallery on the first floor where everyone lived, well above flood-level. Not that the Mississippi gave too many problems now that the levées—the banks—had been raised so high.

A soft sigh left her lips. It might be called Steamboat Gothic by some people, but it was the most beautiful house she'd ever seen. She longed to discover what he'd done inside.

'Stay,' he coaxed. 'You know you want to. Stay as long as it takes. I'll pay your salary and more.' His voice throbbed seductively. 'Think of this as a situation needing your tact and diplomacy. You're used to coping with difficult people in your job. Why not go transatlantic?'

There was, she thought, a difference. Here she was in danger of losing the tough outer skin she'd grown, and it had taken her years to layer it on so that it was virtually impenetrable. 'I have just two weeks' holiday. It's not that easy——'

'It never is,' he muttered. 'But any woman who is a trouble-shooter can handle Melanie...' His mouth quirked. 'And me. You know you can't turn down the offer. You have to do this. How can you abandon the child? You, her godmother, with her interests at heart?'

'Find an au pair,' she said, twisting her hands, every bone in her body urging her to say yes, yes! 'Get in touch with an agency. My life is mapped out——'

'All roads lead to Tom?' he suggested sardonically. 'Take a detour off the route.'

'I am worried about her welfare, I grant you.' She tried to be careful of exposing her longing. How wonderful it would be, she thought wistfully.

'You English are so damn good with kids,' he murmured, his hand brushing back tendrils of her hair from her forehead.

She quivered, alive to his caress, fighting against the humiliating desire. 'Chance, you know perfectly well I can't stay here with you while Annie's in the clinic.'

'I'd sleep in one of the outbuildings. Perhaps the old bachelor quarters. That would be most suitable, wouldn't it?' he asked in a teasing tone. 'The choice is,' he continued ruthlessly, 'your reputation and a delayed return home, versus my daughter's happiness. Do you want a complete stranger caring for her? Have you seen the damage done so far? I have my work to do. I can't be with her all the time. Is your boyfriend more important than your godchild?'

'That's unfair,' she complained.

'So it is. I'm interested that you even hesitate.'

She set her mouth grimly. 'Brute.'

'I'm fighting for what I love,' he said simply. Rosalind's eyes widened and lifted to his. He seemed deadly serious suddenly. 'You could save her, Ros,' he coaxed. 'You could turn her into the sweet child she really is, with your mix of common sense, laughter and straight-from-the-shoulder wisdom. It comes naturally to you.

She responds to you as she's done with no one else. You don't have a choice, really, do you?'

And there was the distraught Annie, running up the steps now and slamming open the full-length white jalousies leading into one of the rooms above, more concerned for her own self than her daughter—her *fostered* daughter, thought Rosalind with a destructive mental anguish.

She saw Melanie racing back towards the car, her dark hair flying behind her, elation on her face, and her heart warmed to see her. This is my child, she thought, with a secret thrill in saying it, even though it was only to herself. For a short while, I can have a hand in caring for her. Tucking her up at night. Cuddling her. Storing memories.

She swallowed hard. 'It would be unwise,' she whispered, wavering.

'Since when was it the rule to be wise?' He smiled at her gentle, flushed face. 'Stop crawling blindly through life. You're missing the excitement. Throw yourself over the cliff, Ros. See what kind of place lies beyond.'

She knew already. A swamp, and she'd be up to her neck and struggling in its muddy waters before she even started drowning. She lifted her head and sniffed the musky smell drifting from the river and with it the scent of roses and warm, moist earth. The smell of Louisiana. She loved it and all it contained.

'I'll stay,' Rosalind whispered, her heart unfolding to her approaching child. 'Temporarily. For a short while. I'll stay,' she mumbled, aghast at her foolhardiness.

'Good. You won't regret it,' said Chance in an expressionless voice.

I will, she thought; I know without any shadow of doubt that I will.

Rosalind slid from the car as Melanie ran full tilt into her. She swung the child around, laughing and feeling free as a bird. But she wasn't. She bit her lip. She mustn't get to love this child too much. Melanie belonged to Annie. Annie and Chance.

And not only was it in Melanie's interests that they be a family unit again, it was Rosalind's duty to her friend to get them all back together. In Chance's eyes, she was only a stop-gap till Annie was better.

His arm dropped casually around her shoulders and she didn't shrug it off because she wanted Melanie to see her father as a friend, not as an enemy. It was important that Chance be built up in Melanie's estimation. When she left, he had to take on the burden of being strong enough for all three of them.

'Did you say something about supper? Someone ought to warn Kate,' said Rosalind breathlessly.

'Melanie will.'

'Shan't.'

Rosalind's restraining hand stopped Chance's angry retort. 'Now who else here can run as fast as you? You could see what's on the menu and come back to tell us before we've reached the house,' she suggested to the little girl in a conspiratorial way. 'I wonder if you've got any jambalaya?' she said wistfully. 'Oh, I've *longed* for that.'

'I'm going to see!' Melanie scrambled free from Rosalind's arms. 'I've gone!' she yelled over her shoulder, racing over the coarse grass to the old overseer's house where Kate lived.

'That was well done. I'm going to speak to Annie,' said Chance softly, turning Rosalind around to face him. 'You take yourself off to the guest-room at the end of the gallery and freshen up.'

'But——'

His finger pressed against her lips. 'No buts. You've committed yourself. You can't back out.' His eyes simmered and she felt a twinge of unease. 'One of the maids can take your key to the hotel and pack your things then get them brought over here.' His mouth briefly followed where his finger had touched, in a light, fluttering kiss. 'Thank you.'

'Chance,' she said hoarsely. 'Don't think——'

'Who, me? I prefer action,' he smiled.

There was a brief moment when the light in his eyes warned her of his intentions but she was so off guard that she didn't make sense of it until too late. By then he had pulled her roughly into his strong, male body and was kissing her with all the passion of a fevered lover, raining kisses on her face, her neck, her throat...

'No, no!' she cried angrily.

'We've been through all that,' he said, his hand sliding between them to the swell of her voluptuous breasts. 'And come out the other side. You told me in the car that you want to wipe out the mistakes, that it's never too late, that you want to forget the past and live for the present——'

'What?' she breathed in horror. 'You misunderstood what I was saying! If you thought I was making myself available——'

'Aren't you?'

'No!' she moaned, turning her head in a futile attempt to escape his searching mouth.

'Cut out the coyness,' he rasped. 'Don't play out this game of cat-and-mouse. You want me.'

'I won't be used as a sex-toy for your gratification! It's not me that has to forgive and forget, it's you and Annie! I meant that I want you two and Melanie to get back together!'

He froze. And released her, his face as cold and hard as permafrost. The black, inscrutable eyes narrowed. 'Happy families,' he growled. 'God, Rosalind! Are you *blind*?'

Savagely he strode away, thundering up the wooden steps and along the open gallery, and Rosalind despaired. Chance didn't believe that Annie would ever forgive him for his infidelity. She must give him hope.

Melanie desperately needed the security and love of a family.

She heard the violent crash above as Chance flung open the louvred french doors to the master bedroom. Then came Chance's angry voice. She began to run. He'd looked ready to kill someone.

'Out!' he roared, when Rosalind dashed breathlessly into the bedroom.

Her eyes took in the silent, sullen Annie sitting on the bed and Chance glowering over her, his legs astride, arms dangling by his sides and fists clenching ominously. She saw the chaotic disarray of clothes and flew to the aid of her friend, pushing Chance to one side and confronting him boldly.

'Don't you bully her! Pick on someone as tough as you!' she rasped, her voice shaking with anger.

'I did,' he growled. 'She said no.' His dark eyes glittered cruelly.

Rosalind winced. She understood the rage that consumed him. Of wanting and believing you'd never be happy. She felt it too. But he had to understand that seeking comfort in another woman's arms wasn't the way out.

'Oh, Chance!' she said sorrowfully. 'Can't you see, you're destroying the only chance of happiness you have——?'

He caught her shoulders and shook her, once, then released her when her chest heaved and she looked as though she was going to defend herself with her bare fists. 'Damn you, Rosalind!' he said savagely. 'Consider your actions and your conclusions before you leap into the fray. You're the one who's just thrown away a promising future.'

'You arrogant devil!' she said, white-lipped. Carefully she reined in her temper. He was beside himself because he loved Annie and was lashing out like a trapped animal at anyone in his path, blindly wreaking vengeance on

the whole world. 'Don't bait me,' she said unsteadily.
'I know what you really feel.'

'I doubt it,' he answered cynically. 'You'd never have
the imagination.'

Her temper simmered and was checked. 'I think I
understand something about the pain and pleasure of
love,' she said bravely, meeting his unreadable eyes.

'From Tom? You do surprise me.' Abruptly he turned
his back on her. 'Now, if you don't mind, I want to talk
to my ex-wife before I explode. Tell her, Annabel!'

The use of her full name seemed to jerk Annie into
life. 'It's OK, Ros,' she said wearily. 'I know I have to
talk to Chance. I have to tell him.'

Rosalind's heart stilled. 'Tell him...what?' she
whispered.

Annie gave an imperceptible shake of her head to reassure her. 'That I must go away.'

Mingled with Rosalind's relief was a new anxiety. She
gave a sympathetic sigh and sat on the bed. 'You can't
run from your feelings,' she said gently. 'Your problems
follow you. I know that.'

'I must go. Please understand. I need treatment!' said
Annie quietly. 'I'd like your help, Ros.'

'Oh, Annie! You have it!' She took Annie's bony hand
in hers and after a moment she felt the pressure increase
till it was almost unbearable. Her friend needed help
and support desperately, she thought with tender compassion. 'Annie,' she said brokenly. 'Oh, Annie.' She
cuddled her dear friend in her arms, rocking her as if
she were a child while Chance stood by woodenly, his
face anguished. And her heart went out to both of them.
Both in love with one another, both too proud to say
so, violently at odds.

'Don't be nice to me,' muttered Annie. 'I don't deserve it.'

'Of course you do!' Rosalind leant back and smiled
at the pinched face. 'Look at what you did for me.' To

her astonishment, Annie began to cry. 'Oh, you two! Why don't you *talk* about this? I beg you both to stop being so proud and stubborn. Tell her your feelings,' she implored Chance. 'She needs to know.'

'You're making things worse,' he said huskily. 'Look at Annie's face. You're tearing her apart for reasons you're totally unaware of. Leave it, Ros!' he finished, with a glare.

'I'm sorry,' said Rosalind quietly, wishing they'd be honest with one another. They must have had a terrible row to have created all this bitter animosity. She put aside her own pain. 'But you must see that Melanie needs the stability of a settled home life.'

Chance's eyes closed and he inhaled deeply. 'You and I have to talk, Annie.'

His sharp white teeth bared in a brief grimace and he ignored Rosalind as if she weren't there. She thought that at least they were communicating at last. She tried not to feel miserable but it was no use and an over-whelming sense of sadness filled her mind and body.

'I want Ros to care for Melanie.' Calmer now, Annie fixed her eyes solemnly on his. 'I know I need professional help. I've tried to keep going because up to now there's been no one around I could trust. The au pairs couldn't handle Melly. Ros could.'

'But Annie, you could have asked Chance to help,' frowned Rosalind.

'Melanie and I became estranged,' said Chance curtly.

How sad, thought Rosalind. 'Well, he's decided to stay at the plantation, you'll be pleased to hear, so that situation will soon change,' she said confidently. 'We'll all look after Melanie, don't worry about that.' She managed a grin. 'I'll train Chance up. By the time I have to go back to England, he'll be able to cope.'

Inwardly she felt troubled as she looked at Annie because she wasn't sure it would be that easy. Chance would have his work cut out. She knew how long the treatment would take.

'But I want you to have her,' said Annie. 'You'd care for her better. You take her,' she said. 'Please. I'd feel better if you did. Permanently.'

'What?' gasped Rosalind.

'By heaven! Over my dead body!' roared Chance. 'She's my child! Are you mad?'

Pain was robbing Rosalind of breath. She wanted her child more than anything. Yet she had to deny that need or Chance would begin to suspect Annie's reason for abandoning Melanie to her 'godmother'. 'Chance, make allowances! Annie's not well. She thinks—she thinks——'

'I know what she thinks,' he growled.

'Look, Annie, love,' implored Rosalind. 'This is Melanie's home; it's all she knows. She said she never wanted to leave. You don't know what you're say-ing——'

'You must take her, you must!' wailed Annie.

'Oh, no, no, don't ask me to do this; you can't!' Rosalind said unhappily. Hardening her heart, she forced herself to betray her love for Melanie. 'Heavens, how could I, what with my job and Tom—he'd have a fit if I turned up with a seven-year-old child!' she said in mock alarm, clamping hard on the hysteria surging up inside.

Annie was looking at her with disappointment. Let her think I'm cold-hearted, thought Rosalind. Annie must be made to turn to Chance for help and love.

'I don't know you any more,' said Annie, her eyes hard and unfriendly. 'I thought...I thought—well, you know, that you'd be a better mother than me.' Her eyes were puzzled.

Rosalind smiled brightly in amused amazement. Too brightly. She earned a blistering glare of contempt from Chance when she began to elaborate. 'Motherhood isn't natural to every woman. Even if it were possible, I'd

find it hard after all this time to give up my freedom,'
she said with a forced laugh, as if she was humouring
an invalid. 'It's OK for a short time to play godmother,
but how would I manage if I had to do it forever?'

The harsh lines marked Chance's face. 'There. You
have her answer. You and I will work something out,
Annie, when you're better.'

Annie averted her eyes. 'Ros, you'll stay with Melanie
until you're not needed, won't you?'

'I will,' said Rosalind, her smile wavering.

'Then let me and Chance talk. He and I have a few
things to sort out.'

'Are you sure you'll be all right with him?' asked
Rosalind quietly.

'Sweet hallelujah!' muttered Chance in a rolling growl.
Rosalind hesitated. 'You've been asked to leave,' he said
curtly. 'Go and give Melanie her supper and get her to
bed.'

'I...' She balked at obeying his order. But it was one
she wanted to carry out. Annie's confidence had been
convincing enough. And perhaps she should leave them
to discuss Melanie's future—and theirs. 'All right. Tell
her your real feelings, Chance.'

'I intend to clarify them,' he said grimly.

'I'm so glad,' she said, astonished that her voice
wavered as if she was about to cry. Disconcerted by the
strength of her emotions, she whirled around and left
them to it.

Her time with Melanie was sweet and sour. Her
daughter had no table manners and Rosalind itched to
show her how to behave, but restrained herself. Time
enough for that later. She bit her lip. How much later?
How long? The more she stayed, the deeper she'd fall
for her child.

After a no-holds-barred bath, Rosalind admired the
star on the bedroom door and allowed herself to be
taught a few simple ballet positions by her graceful

daughter before she read Melanie a story, stroking the child's hair gently until she fell asleep. For a long time Rosalind just sat there staring through the draped mosquito net, drinking in every scrap of the sweet features, imprinting them on her mind. One day all she'd have would be her memories and she wanted the images to be sharp enough to last for eternity.

She felt the tears rolling down her cheeks and let them fall unchecked, the heaviness of her heart too great to bear any longer.

CHAPTER FOUR

'I WANT you in my study.'

Rosalind's drooping head lifted slowly at Chance's husky growl. 'Just a minute,' she croaked, leaning forwards and kissing Melanie's soft cheek. It smelt of baby powder and made her even more miserable.

'You're crying.'

'I'm not!' she denied hotly, but her eyes continued to fill with treacherous proof that she was lying.

Chance impatiently caught hold of her hand and drew her out to the wide, airy gallery. There, she was immediately assailed by the warmth of the southern night, the cicadas whirring in the undergrowth, the soft swish of the fans overhead and the faint, evocative perfume of wild herbs released into the air.

And her shoulders began to shake with her hopeless weeping.

'Ros——'

'Leave—me—alone!' she blurted out between jagged sobs. She wanted to be miserable. Annie had offered her the chance to take Melanie away, to love her for always, and nothing would ever compensate for the fact that she would have to turn her back on her own flesh and blood and walk away. 'I hate you, I hate you, hate you!' she ground out through her teeth.

He leant against a graceful white column and, despite her protests, quickly drew her to him and held her close. Her emotions torn to shreds, she sobbed silently into the soft cloth of his tuxedo.

'Interesting,' he drawled, rocking her a little. 'All those protests of hatred. Whatever are you crying about? Annie will get better soon. I know she's your friend and this has brought back memories of a bad time in your life, but really!'

Panicking, not daring to trust herself, Rosalind said the first thing that came into her head. 'I don't want to stay here for months. I loathe you. You've trapped me. I—I want to get back to—to Tom. You of all people must appreciate what it's like being kept in a prison.'

'You don't know the meaning of the word,' he said savagely. 'You don't know what it's like to wake up every morning and know it will be the same as the day before and the day before that, and that ahead stretches hours and hours of total boredom without human company. You learn a few things about yourself in prison, Rosalind.'

'Not compassion,' she sniffed, wishing she didn't feel such a great deal of sympathy for him. He'd served the sentence. Yet the thought of the tough, physical and energy-fired Chance in a confined space was terrible.

Her imagination absurdly placed him at a barred window, his dark—probably bearded—face gaunt and harrowed as he stared out at the sunshine, and she scolded herself for being such a melodramatic idiot. They probably had TV and en-suite bathrooms, she thought sulkily, looking up at him. He had been swaying with her gently, as if remembering, and his malevolent, vengeful expression scared her.

'You discard compassion after a week,' he said tightly. 'An experience like that hardens you.' The secretive eyes scanned her upturned face. 'It makes you want to grab everything you've ached for while you've been inside.' Brutally he pushed her from him and she breathed a sigh of relief. 'So don't moan to me about your so-called prison just because your nice little plans for a nice little future have been messed around and you can't see a way out.'

'I got a bit homesick,' she said huskily, dabbing at her eyes. Chance's cruel gaze seemed fixed to her trembling mouth. Hastily she clamped her lips shut and he responded with a mocking smile.

'No other reason?' he asked.

'What could there be?' she dissembled.

'Then you needn't make such a fuss.' He smiled innocently at her indignant pout. 'All I'm asking is that you help out for a while till Melanie's used to me,' he murmured. 'Then I'll be able to manage, with Kate's help, till Annie is better. She and I have cleared the air between us. I think that'll help her.'

Calmed by his steady voice, she dabbed at her tear-stained face. 'It was a messy divorce?' she asked.

'Worse beforehand,' he said darkly. 'The atmosphere between us could have been cut by a chain-saw. Don't make judgements when you only know half the story.'

'Then tell me the whole story,' she demanded.

His dark, glowing eyes assessed her and she shifted uncomfortably, lifting her graceful head in an attitude of challenge. A faint smile lifted the corners of his lips. 'You say that you loathe me.'

'Yes,' she said sullenly.

He took a step towards her and her breathing quickened. 'That'll do,' he drawled. 'It's more convenient that way.'

Warily she backed off, till her spine hit the balustrade. 'What do you mean, it'll do? What's more convenient?' she said, tossing her head with a hauteur she didn't feel.

'You won't fall in love with me,' he said calmly.

'Darn tootin' I won't!' she spluttered. 'Now go away. I don't want you to touch me,' she snapped.

'Is that so?' he said, raising unbelieving eyebrows. 'I want to know what you've been doing all these years,' he murmured. 'Whether you've thought of me, of that moment by the river and if you ever had any regrets. Because for that short time we were together we were quite sensational.' He paused a short distance from her, his expression suspiciously tender. 'I will look after you, Rosalind. Would you like that? I will take care of you and you will want for nothing while you're here...' He smiled. 'For as long as you stay.'

His fingers whispered in a light caress over her forehead and traced her brows. Still emotionally shaken and confused, battered by events, she closed her eyes, feeling his touch on them, her senses lurching. She wanted him to hold her so very much. Weak with longing, she clung to him, needing—for once in her life—someone to take away all the pain, of having to be strong and dependable. She tried not to think, to blank out everything, because she was so tired of fighting her way in the world.

'No, please don't, Chance,' she said hastily. The last few years had been a tremendous strain. She needed love as much as Melanie did.

'I want you,' he whispered. 'So much that I can hardly breathe when I think of it.'

She went rigid, horrified that he'd misunderstood why she was letting him comfort her. Or was she? An instinct for self-preservation blazed a warning. 'No,' she said harshly. With supreme confidence, he slid his hands to her waist and her body arched into his languorously before she could stop it. The cicadas seemed to whirr faster, the perfumes grow headier. 'Chance,' she grated, half drunk with the sensual slide of his fingers. 'Oh, Chance...'

She gasped, her jacket apparently open, his hands already spilling out her breasts.

'Oh, God! Rosalind!' he groaned hoarsely, looking, touching, tormenting her with his remorseless desire. 'You're gorgeous. Quite gorgeous. You've become even more of a woman. So beautiful...'

He seemed unable to speak, wordlessly watching her while he stroked the smooth curves of her hot skin. She tried not to will him to go on and satisfy her deep, wanton need. Somehow she must persuade her paralysed hands to move now and cover up her nakedness.

'No. Don't touch me——' She drove her teeth into her lip as he lightly feathered his fingers over the high swell of her breasts, tantalisingly avoiding their throbbing twin centres.

'I must. I'm compelled. Where of all this glory shall I explore now?' he murmured softly. 'Here...? Here...? Perhaps...here.' His fingers paused on the gentle curve of her hip and wandered back to rest lightly on her ribs. 'Are you as aroused as I am, Rosalind? Is that why your breathing is so harsh? Tell me. Talk to me. Show me where you ache. Touch me. Let all those inhibitions go and give yourself as you did before. Have you ever been any nearer perfect unity than on that day?'

'I—I——' She closed her anguished eyes. Two fore-fingers had brushed across each rosy peak of her breasts. She and Chance gave a simultaneous involuntary shudder and in the darkness Rosalind could feel her breasts straining and knew her nipples were growing harder and harder beneath his exquisite torture. A small sound of pleasure fluttered in her throat and, before she knew it, she was responding with a deep groan, unable to help herself.

'Sweet heaven!' Chance growled hoarsely.

Rosalind threw back her head. Chance's mouth de-scended possessively on her throat, savaging it with sweet, gentle restraint, the pains of need stabbing re-peatedly inside her till she felt she might swoon. Her arms twined around his neck and they looked at one another for a long, timeless moment.

Helpless, she caught handfuls of his hair in her fists and drove his mouth down on hers, demanding that he should lose control, trying to ease from her body all the emptiness of the past years without him.

I love him, she thought wildly. It's crazy. But I still love him, whatever he is, whatever he does.

With a groan, he swept her into his arms. 'I should have done this a long time ago,' he said harshly.

'Oh, no,' she whispered, her eyes enormous in the darkness. She meant yes. Of course she did. Sense and decency were making her refuse. But the wildness that had possessed her when she was in New Orleans and in Chance's arms was fiercer and he knew that at a glance.

Like a summer tornado, he whirled into action, whisking her along the gallery to the guest-room before she could draw breath to contradict herself again. 'This time,' he muttered grimly, 'you won't get away.'

He threw her on the bed and flung himself down with her, tearing off her jacket, wrenching at her skirt zip and sensuously, oh, so utterly sensuously, slithering it down her thighs and hurling it somewhere into the darkness behind him.

In a daze, she lifted her arms and feebly remonstrated with him, her limbs quite leaden and uncontrollable. Because her body knew what it wanted. Chance Decatur—that impure but totally satisfying lover. The father of my child, she thought hazily to herself. And let out a great moan of despair.

'Not long, sweetheart,' breathed Chance raggedly.

'Oh, no, no, no!' she groaned, and, like lightning, rolled to the edge of the bed and shakily stood up, clutching at the drapes of the half-tester for support. 'I can't, you can't—— Oh, Chance!' she choked, lifting one corner of the bedspread to cover her nakedness. How had that happened? She blinked in confusion. 'You're so disgustingly clever at getting women out of their clothes!' she whispered accusingly.

'Hey, Ros——'

She looked down on his dark head, the black brows now beetling together angrily. He'd been rejected. She gave a small, ironic laugh. That was what she'd planned earlier. And now it had really happened. For a woman to refuse him at this stage must be humiliating in the extreme to him. That was how she must play it. Dangerous. But it might save her from being touched again. Another time she might take the brief gratification and regret it for the rest of her life.

Never, ever would she let him make love to her. 'Unpleasant, isn't it?' she said hoarsely, slowly regaining control of her brain. Her legs, though, were another matter. 'Think of all the women you've let down,' she grated through clenched teeth, denying her throbbing pulses. 'This is for Annie and all of them. This is for all the women in the future. Remember well how it feels. A sense of loss, of hollowing emptiness. And humiliating shame, as if something's unfinished. It feels cheap and nasty, doesn't it? Leaves a sour taste in the mouth.'

His face had become as cold as ice. 'You bitch. You vicious little witch! So that was why you came back,' he said with sinister softness. 'Revenge. Don't you know that vengeance always turns back on the avenger?'

His arm shot out and she stumbled on to the bed again. But this time Chance was in deadly earnest, taking no notice of her pleas, her moans, her frantically struggling body.

'Chance, this is not the way...not with such hatred——'

His dark, fathomless eyes glinted in the darkness as he hovered over her naked, pinioned figure. 'You owe me this,' he said thickly, his fingers insolently trailing over her thigh. And she realised in terror that he was beyond listening to sense, driven by animal lust and his dangerous ego. 'You said yes to me. You aroused me, you gambled in the most dangerous game I know. And you have just lost.'

His kiss obliterated her protest. It filled her mind with its insistence till she could think of nothing else, only that sweet taste of his lips, his warmth, his passion. His voice murmured in her ear. She felt his mouth on its folds, on her throat, the ridge of her collarbone. His hands began to weave a magic of their own and all the time he was talking to her, words describing her body in the most sensual terms, words which in her madness she wanted to hear and to savour because there had been no pleasure like this in her life since Sans Souci.

'I don't want this,' she managed in a throaty whisper, afraid of his potential violence. Yet . . . there was gentleness in his touch as if he was in control.

'Yes, you do,' he said ruthlessly. 'Look down at your breasts. Look how dark they are . . . here . . .' She gasped, as his mouth told her where. 'I can touch you and see your body leap into life and I know that you want me with the same desperation that we both felt that day on the banks of the river.'

'No,' she moaned. 'I refuse to——'

'Refuse all you like,' he said brutally. 'It won't make any difference.'

His kisses took her by storm. And then they gentled, becoming persuasive and coaxing, the movement of his hands on her body slow and infinitely seductive. And it was that, the tenderness—however false—that broke her will-power.

Someone to love her. Someone to care—even if it was with an ulterior motive . . . Hungry for affection, for Chance's love, she felt herself moving against his body, melting in his arms, her mouth lifting to kiss his.

'Say you want me,' he whispered. 'That you want me to caress you like a lover. That you desire me.'

His sultry eyes looked deeply into hers. He smiled gently, and in her stupid longing she told herself it was a tender look. But she couldn't bring herself to speak.

Lightly he kissed her, his fingers sliding to her thighs. She closed her eyes and lay rigid, refusing to allow the gentle movements to affect her. But Chance was too skilled a lover and she began to gasp, then clutched at him, her eyes determinedly shut so that she wouldn't see the triumph she knew must be on his face.

And then he stopped. She moaned. He didn't move. Her head lifted to present her lips to him but still he made no move. Her body arched provocatively so that her breasts brushed against his firmly muscled chest. A shudder ran through him but he did nothing.

It had been too long since he'd touched her where she most wanted. The throbbing was too urgent; to her shame, it had taken over her whole existence. Distressed, she opened her eyes and felt a kick of unbelievable need in her stomach at the way he was looking at her.

'Oh, Chance,' she whispered. Her hips rose in demand. 'Please . . .' She gulped at the way his tongue slicked over his lips. Then he touched her, so delicately that it was like the drift of a butterfly's wing. Her body jerked in response.

Then, his face strangely closed, he drew back and began to dress.

'What . . . what . . . ?' Her voice petered out.

His gleaming, sweat-slicked back somehow managed to look angry. 'Your lesson, Rosalind. Don't play your smart games on me again,' he said in a savage growl. 'Next time, so help me, I'll destroy you even if it destroys me in the process.'

A groan flew from her lips, a terrible shudder of wanting. 'Chance,' she began through cracked lips.

'No,' he grated, whirling around to scowl at her. 'I don't need you to appease my hunger. I'll damn well go elsewhere.'

The room fell silent. His eyes bored into hers as if he was thinking of challenging her to a duel in no man's land down the center of Canal Street, where all hot-

blooded French aristocrats had met and fought anyone
who insulted their pride.

Rosalind drew in a long, shaking breath. 'You devil!'
she breathed, her eyes showing how terribly hurt she was.

'If I am, you've made me one,' he said coldly. 'No
woman gets the better of me. I fight as dirty as you,
Rosalind. Don't ever forget that. I'll get what I want—
your total submission. You'll be eager and willing by the
time I've finished with you. You'll come crawling to me
along the length of Oak Alley whenever I snap my
fingers.'

'I won't!' she whispered, appalled.

'Don't take bets,' he snarled. 'You will crawl, sweetheart. And crawl and crawl again till I want nothing more
of you.'

His face utterly remorseless, he buttoned his shirt,
found his tie and angrily flicked it around his neck. When
he reached down for his discarded tuxedo, Rosalind gave
an involuntary quiver, the glorious lines of his body
making her limbs melt.

'No!' she cried. 'You'll get arthritis in your fingers
from snapping them before I do what you say, because
I'll be leaving in the morning!'

'Oh, no, you won't.' Straightening, he stood menacingly at the foot of the bed, a broad-shouldered pagan
male in the clothes of a civilised businessman—the savage
beneath the thin worldly veneer. 'If you leave, I go. That
was the deal. United we stand—or crawl, in your case.
Divided, we get on with our dreary lives without the hin-
drance of a child.'

Her eyes widened and she called his bluff. 'I don't
believe you'd leave Melanie on her own——'

'No? I can and I will,' he said with steely determination. 'Why should I stay?'

Rosalind's mouth opened and closed. 'You're her
father!'

He shrugged. 'So what? She's been running wild these last few months; what difference will it make if she does for a few more? Kate will feed her and Blanche will educate her in the ways of men. She'll be perfectly worthy of your sex by the time she grows up.'

'You cynical swine! How can you be so indifferent to your own child's fate?' she cried angrily.

'Because I'm a callous bastard!' he roared, his tone lashing her with fury. 'I cheat the elderly out of their homes for the sake of a quick profit, remember? Of course,' he added harshly, 'I might stay. I might decide to train Melanie to be cold and hard like me, ruthless, efficient enough to take on my business and run it with the same complete lack of human emotion that I do! I ought to start now, if I'm leaving everything to her.'

Rosalind's hand flew to her mouth. 'You wouldn't deliberately set out to mould her into a heartless machine!'

His mouth twisted. 'No? You'll never be sure if you go, will you?' he said with soft savagery.

'Oh, God!' muttered Rosalind dully. He could be bluffing. But if he wasn't...

'I never thought you were chicken,' he challenged.

'I'm not!' she scowled. 'But the thought of being near you is so unpleasant——' She grimaced.

'Annie's relying on you,' he said coldly. 'She's agreed to go to a clinic in Dallas and I've booked her in on the morning flight. Without you here, she won't go; she said so. Why would that be, Rosalind?'

'Because she knows that you wouldn't give your daughter much of a time, I expect,' she muttered.

'Go home if you want,' he said with callous indifference. 'But if you do Annie won't get treated and Melanie will become a carbon copy of me. I swear it. I'm damned if I'm letting men hurt her because she's vulnerable. I'll make her tough, to stand the knocks, to give as good as she gets.'

'You're blackmailing me!' she accused indignantly.

'Yes.'

She blinked at the blatant admission. 'You can't expect me to stay after—after assaulting me!' she cried, astounded.

He smiled sardonically. 'Why not? It didn't mean anything to you, did it?'

Horrified, she watched him leave and slam the door with no thought or care for anyone in the house. Her body began to shake and she curled up like a child in the huge bed, staring sightlessly into space, numb at the thought of what was to come.

Every minute spent near Chance was increasingly dangerous—let alone *days*. He had the look of a man determined to get the upper hand and, in Chance's case, that always meant sexual domination.

It was the most awful situation. And it could go on for months. Rosalind groaned, trying to think how she could persuade Chance to think of Melanie's needs, not his own—and certainly not to experiment with his cynical ideas of turning his daughter into someone as cold-hearted as her father.

'We're cookin' breakfast, you and me!'

'Urrrgh.' Rosalind struggled awake to find Melanie treating her bed like a trampoline. 'Oh, lor',' she mumbled.

'Hash browns...warm muffins...Cajun omelette...!' yelled Melanie in time to the bounces.

'Good grief!' she groaned. 'I need peace and quiet, not a circus act. Give me a cuddle instead and let me discover if I can make my eyes open a bit more or if someone's glued them together.'

The door burst open. Chance, unusually dishevelled, appeared to be still in the clothes he'd worn the previous night. 'What the devil——?' He stopped in mid-sentence when he saw the intimate scene, his face set like granite.

'We're cuddlin',' said Melanie defiantly, her arms around Rosalind's neck in a death-hug.

His eyes flickered. 'Can't you do it without all that racket?' he asked quietly.

But over Melanie's dark head Rosalind had seen the brief warmth in his eyes and the longing. That gave her more hope than she'd expected. She had to start getting these two together as fast as humanly possible and the bond between them would do the rest. Then she could go. She whispered to Melanie, 'Say good morning to your father. Go and give him a cuddle, too.'

'Shan't.'

'You a coward?' challenged Rosalind slyly.

'No, I'm not!' She rolled on to her back beside Rosalind. 'You gotta cuddle for your only daughter?' she wheedled, opening her small arms.

Chance's mouth twitched, his eyes mocking. 'Not quite what you intended, was it?' he drawled smoothly, strolling over, lithe and feral, a devastatingly superior smile on his face.

Trapped in the bed, all Rosalind could do was to suffer his inclusive embrace. Melanie nuzzled up to him, laughing at his dark stubble, running her soft fingers over it, wondering wickedly if it would scour pans cheaper than the products Kate used. To Rosalind it was the ultimate irony, the three of them in a loving family embrace. And she was the only one who knew they were a family at all.

'You're heavy,' she muttered in his ear, suddenly unable to bear having him sprawled over her any longer.

'You never used to say that,' he husked, his face too close for normal breathing. But he sat up, and held Melanie's shoulders firmly, looking at his daughter solemnly. 'Mommy wants to see you,' he said gently. 'She's not feeling well and she's having a few days in hospital while a doctor works out what's wrong.'

'Oh. Poor Mommy. She's been ill a lot. Can I visit?' asked Melanie anxiously.

Rosalind sat up a little higher, tucking the sheet securely around her naked body, and put her arms around her daughter. 'Can she? Can we?' she asked Chance.

'Not to begin with,' he answered curtly. 'Not till they know the cause for sure and then it'll be a while. Melly, you will have to be the lady of the house in her place and——'

'Me, a lady?' she squawked.

He grinned his heart-stopping grin. 'Yes,' he said laconically. 'It strikes me as unlikely, too.'

'It's not that funny,' said Melanie, bristling. 'Why isn't Ros goin' to be the lady of the house?'

His glance wandered over Rosalind, her dark hair tumbling over the big pillows, her smooth, naked shoulders gleaming a soft gold in the morning sun. 'Well, she could be the mistress,' he mused, his mouth twitching at Rosalind's glare. 'But at the moment she's our guest.'

'Blanche says she's your mistress,' frowned Melanie. 'Does that mean she's the same as Rosalind, or is she in charge?'

Chance smiled wryly at Rosalind's horrified face and then dabbed his daughter's nose with a playful finger. 'You hear too much gossip. And no mistress of mine would ever be in charge. I'm always the boss, Melanie. You're the hostess. Can you be that? It's an awful responsibility for someone as young as you.'

Rosalind hid a faint smile at his cunning. She might not have to work too hard at helping the relationship along after all.

'Course I can do it. I can do anything I want,' said Melanie solemnly, her eyes so like Chance's that Rosalind smiled.

He hesitated, then leaned forwards and kissed Melanie fondly. 'Thanks, pal. You're terrific,' he said softly and Rosalind's mouth trembled. 'When you've seen Mommy,

I want you and Kate to plan the meals for the next few days and help her by going shopping. I'm going to shave. I'll see you two at breakfast.'

He left them. Chattering brightly all the time, Rosalind dressed and then coaxed Melanie into showing her how to cook the breakfast, loving every minute of the intimacy between them.

'Smells good,' came his low growl from the doorway. 'Where's Melly?'

'With Annie. She's taken some toast up to her.' Rosalind watched him lift the lids off dishes and help himself to a huge plate of food.

He caught her astonished glance and smiled. 'I'm hungry,' he explained, his eyes teasing. 'My appetite's been stimulated.'

Blushing under his long, assessing look, she tried to compose her scattered poise. 'I'll cook hash browns and eggs-over-easy for you, but that's as far as I'll go to satisfy your appetite,' she said tightly.

'Would you deny a starving man?' he murmured.

She eyed the half-eaten chorizo sausage on his plate. 'You don't know the meaning of the word,' she said sarcastically.

'That's where you're wrong,' he said quietly.

Her hand was arrested in mid-air by the low fervour of his voice. 'You're referring to prison?' she asked. 'If so, you managed to do without the luxuries in life then.'

He shrugged. 'One man's luxury is another man's necessity,' he drawled. 'Besides, then I had no choice.'

'You don't have any now,' she reminded him sharply.

He sipped his coffee, his eyes blazing messages of piratical avarice over the rim of the cup. 'I'm no saint,' he growled. 'Temptation surrounds me.'

'Then I suggest you get a hold on yourself,' snapped Rosalind. 'Don't you care what kind of environment your daughter lives in? Do you have to go around lusting after everything in a skirt?'

'I care,' he said shortly.

'You've not cared for a while,' she said in accusation.

'I'd crucify myself if I ever gave my heart to Melanie.'

'I don't understand! Are you saying you're denying yourself the luxury of loving your own daughter?' exclaimed Rosalind fiercely.

'I'm denying myself the *misery* of loving her,' he corrected. 'It's easier on the emotions if I keep my feelings to myself. Annie and I separated years before we divorced. It was agreed that I'd only see Melanie once a quarter.'

'Why? Couldn't you spare the time?' goaded Rosalind, furious that his needs had come before his daughter's.

'I'm not going into it. I have to live with the fact that my daughter hardly knows me. I resent the situation but I can't change it, or the fact that even the limited access I have gets screwed up by Annie more often than not.'

A great sorrow settled in Rosalind's heart. He'd had a rough time and Annie's lawyer had won highly unfair conditions in the divorce settlement—probably because of Chance's criminal record.

'I'm sorry,' she said sympathetically. She hesitated. 'Chance, your marriage must have been good at the start. In fact I know it was. Annie wrote about the lovely times you'd had together. And I know you still feel something for her. Can't that be rekindled?' added Rosalind shakily, almost mesmerised by his solemn dark eyes, filled with pain.

He frowned. 'No. Don't get me wrong. I admit that she's done a lot for me. It's because of her that my business kept going while I was in prison. And,' he said more gently, 'she gave me my child.'

Rosalind quivered at the emotion in his face. He loved Melanie and that came as a great relief to her. It was ironic that they both were being deprived of their child. And in an odd way he'd hit the nail on the head. Annie *had* given him his child. If it hadn't been for Annie's mistake, Melanie would have been brought up in England and he would never have seen her.

'You have the opportunity to get to know one another better now,' she said huskily. His relationship with his child was the most important thing to get right. 'Show her that you love her and she'll slowly learn to love you even if things seem bleak at the moment.'

'Yes,' he mused. 'OK. If I'm to take time off work, I'll need to make the most of it. We must make sure we all do things together—insist on it, in your own sweet-tough way. Deal?'

Her face was radiant at her unexpected success. If nothing else came from this awful situation, the relationship between Melanie and her father would be improved. 'Deal,' she smiled.

Perhaps if she'd known what he was really up to she would have been less overjoyed. For a whole week, Melanie was infuriating, delightful, wildly uncontrollable and as sweet as a lamb. Chance remained calm, gentle and steadfastly loyal towards his daughter as if he'd taken Rosalind's advice to heart.

Seeing him with his child, Rosalind continually found the anguish within her hard to bear and the poignancy of the situation was not lost on her. Happy families. If he only knew!

Slowly, inexorably, she was being bonded by love more and more strongly to her daughter. And, just as certainly, Chance was showing her how charming and what a wonderful companion he could be. He was doing it again—seducing her before she noticed soon enough to stop the insidious magnetism of his personality from overwhelming her. She was falling headlong in love and in her heart of hearts she knew she never wanted to leave Sans Souci, Melanie, or Chance, ever again.

The evenings were the worst time. Like now, she thought, looking at Chance from beneath her lashes down the length of the gleaming mahogany table. Melanie had gone to bed, and there was no sound in the room other than the woosh of the swaying punkah above the table, the heavy cypress board stirring the sultry air.

Chance lifted his glass, the cut crystal glinting in the soft glowing light from the candelabra. 'To you,' he smiled. 'For turning Melanie into a little girl again in the space of one week. Thank you.'

'You do love her, don't you?' she asked anxiously.

'Yes. Very, very much,' he said solemnly.

Shaken by his feeling, she absently dipped her spoon into the fluffy meringue of her bread pudding and inhaled the sharp aroma of the whisky sauce. She had to escape. Fast.

'I think it would be OK for me to leave now,' she said, her voice threatening to shatter like glass.

It was a long while before he said anything. He cleared his throat. 'Then we ought to have a night out on the town before you do.'

She looked up with a frown, hearing an odd rasp in Chance's voice. But his face was innocent of all guile, and she smiled. For once, she'd do what he wanted, not what she ought. He'd made no move to touch her—all those brief encounters of his hands, his body, his eyes had been accidental, she was sure, because he drew back with a frown every time they had touched.

'Sounds fun,' she said cautiously.

'I'll get Kate over to baby-sit.' Chance rose immediately.

'Oh! I didn't mean now, this minute...' Her hands fluttered to her lap. He thought she was going in the next day or so whereas she'd meant perhaps the end of the week. She bit her lip, to divert her mind from the inevitable wrench of departure. 'Oh, well, why not?' she said with a brittle laugh. 'Am I OK in this?'

His eyes flickered over her demure dress. 'You'll be hot. I was thinking of Bourbon Street, not an air-conditioned hotel dance-floor. What do you think? Something you'll be cool in.'

She nodded and ran to change into the only thing suitable, a backless halter-neck with a swirly skirt. Then she checked Melanie, pausing by the door to smile at the slumbering child.

'Ros? Kate's come.'

'Yes!' She dashed on to the gallery where Chance was waiting.

He grinned when he saw her. 'You look ready to enjoy yourself.'

'I am,' she said with determination. 'Every second. It'll probably be the last time I come here. I want to remember it all.'

'I'd better make sure we don't miss anywhere out,' he murmured. 'We must explore everywhere.'

The soft, warm velvet of the night wrapped around them as they strolled to the garages in the old water tower. Once in New Orleans, the mood changed, and this time when they strolled down the nightly pedestrianised honky-tonk strip along Bourbon Street they were assailed from all sides by noise and lights and the sound of people letting off steam. It was like an all-night party, the jazz searing the air contagious and red-hot, with break-dancers performing beside clowns, Louis Armstrong sound-alikes rasping out the blues in total oblivion to the tap-dancers on the other side of the street.

'Slow-dancing?' suggested Chance, drawing her down a dark alley.

'No, thanks. Get me out of here!' she said in alarm, seeing dim gas-lamps flickering on the narrow cobbled street and sinister men leaning against roughened walls, smoking.

He grinned. 'It's only a club in the old slave quarters,' he murmured, and pulled her into a doorway beneath an ironwork balcony filled with trailing ferns.

'Oh, no, I don't...' Too late, they were inside, his arms were around her and they were dancing. Although it was more like making love, she thought helplessly.

'Enjoy it all,' he murmured. 'Be merry. Tomorrow we die.'

Close, she thought, her cheek against his warm chest. It would be like dying.

The dance-floor was tiny, the music sleazy, the crowds dense, and they did little but shuffle. The movement of his thighs was driving her insane. Being held in his embrace was a wonderful torture that she'd never forget. She heaved a long, soft sigh and put her arms around his neck, enjoying the touch of his fingers on her naked spine.

Each day, each hour, each minute was driving her nearer to the time when she must leave. If she ever stopped to think of that moment, it brought her an intolerable agony.

Eventually she could bear being close to him no more. They walked around the old quarter hand in hand, eating ice-creams and playing tourist till he drove her home, slowly, with the intoxicating sound of a plaintive Cajun love-song whispering all forlorn on the car radio.

'How soon?' he asked quietly, stopping at the beginning of the avenue of evergreen oaks.

She knew what he was referring to. It had been on her mind for a long time. 'After this evening, it ought to be as soon as possible. I don't think I could have as good a time as that again,' she said with a shaky laugh. 'I'll make that my farewell. So... when I can get a flight.'

'Let's walk back.'

Her mind told her not to, her body disobeyed. She slid out of the car and took his hand, big, warm and dry, holding her tightly as if he never wanted to let go. Beneath the oaks it was pitch-dark and a little scary. He drew her close, as if realising her apprehension.

And when he turned her around she didn't object because she wanted the magical evening to go on forever and because in her dreams this was what she wanted: Chance's kisses. His arms around her, enfolding her securely.

'You have the sweetest mouth.'

Half intoxicated by him, she lifted her drowsy lids and smiled. He smiled back at her and they meandered on, arms around one another till they had climbed the steps and were about to enter the upper hall.

'I'll see Kate back to her house,' he said softly. 'And check Melanie.'

'Yes. Thank Kate for me,' husked Rosalind. 'And thank *you*. I've had a lovely evening and I'll always remember it as being something very special. Goodnight, Chance.'

His eyebrow lifted quizzically and she smiled at him, pleased that they would be parting friends. It would make it easier to keep in touch with Melanie. Softly she tiptoed along the gallery to her room and walked through the open doors.

She stretched luxuriously, stripping off her clothes and taking a long, cool shower. Then she padded naked to her half-tester bed in the darkness, drawing aside the heavy fringed drapes and slipping beneath the mosquito sheers.

And saw against the midnight-black sky outside the outline of Chance's powerfully male and sexually alarming body.

CHAPTER FIVE

ROSALIND gasped faintly. In the gloom, she could make out Chance's burning eyes focused menacingly on her. This was her last night and he had nothing to lose. He meant to seduce her.

The big shoulders lifted a little, riveting her eyes. 'I didn't expect you to be in bed,' he said huskily.

'Well, I am,' she breathed, then cleared her throat of its huskiness. 'Goodnight,' she managed, with some cheerfulness in her tone.

'I brought champagne.' He lifted a bottle and two chinking glasses and stepped into the room.

It dawned on her that he wanted to enjoy a slow assault on her senses rather than an outright assault. 'How nice,' she said brightly, deciding to be so chirpy that it would kill the sultry atmosphere stone-dead. Apprehensively she watched him open the champagne with a faint pop, saw the white foam spurting out and filling the glasses. 'What a treat! You're spoiling me!'

Chance lit the old gas-lamp which was fuelled from his own gas supply from beneath the still waters of the blue bayous, and in the flickering soft light she saw how relaxed he looked.

'Here you are, Rosalind.'

Warily she reached under the net to accept her glass and her mouth dried in alarm when he pushed back the folds of the material and sat on the bed. 'I wasn't expecting this,' she said in as close to a conversational tone as she could manage. 'It's a lovely send-off——'

'I thought we'd finish the evening in style,' he smiled. 'A goodbye drink. And I have a present for you.'

'No, please... I don't want presents, not anything——' she demurred hastily.

'I insist,' he answered gently. 'You've done more than
anyone to bring Melanie and me together. No one else
has given a damn. For caring so much, I thank you.'
He raised his glass in a silent toast.

Rosalind smiled, relieved that her suspicions about the
kind of present he was giving her were unfounded. His
tone was too sincere; he was truly grateful. 'Part of a
godmother's job,' she joked cheerfully. 'Waving wands
and all that.'

'Thank you, all the same,' he said warmly. 'I know
you aren't aware of everything that's happened to Annie
and me, but you've put your reservations about me aside
and worked hard to smooth things over. I can't tell you
how grateful I am.'

The emotion in his voice made her feel emotional. 'I
don't like people to be unhappy,' she said quietly. 'I
couldn't stand by and not help.'

'I wanted to give you something that you know I
regard very highly. My relationship with Melanie is
priceless and you have given that to me. How can I match
it with a gift?'

'I'm pleased for you both that you're not estranged
any longer,' she said awkwardly. 'You don't have
to——'

'I do. I want to express what I feel. This is nowhere
near what I owe you, but...' She stared at the box he
had taken from his pocket. It was old and battered, like
a second-hand jewellery box. 'Hold my glass a minute,
would you?' he murmured.

'Chance, really,' she demurred, as he concentrated on
opening the complicated locking device. 'I don't——
Oh!'

He smiled at her gasp of surprise and leant forward,
the Decatur emerald necklace in his hands—the one she'd
seen depicted on the portraits of all the Decatur women

for the last few generations. 'Lean towards me,' he ordered softly, pushing up the net and letting it fall behind him to the floor.

She stayed where she was, her eyes dark and troubled. Men didn't give women expensive jewellery without wanting a lot in return. 'No,' she said unhappily. 'It would be like stealing the family silver. That is an heirloom. The necklace belongs with the Decaturs and should be Melanie's one day. You can't——'

'I can do what I darn well please,' he said easily, laying the necklace against her bare throat. 'My gesture tells you what my child means to me, doesn't it? More than tradition, pride, more than emeralds.'

The necklace hung cold and heavy on her chest, but with Chance leaning over her and a glass of champagne in each hand she could do very little—particularly as she was totally numbed by his action.

'Yes, but I——'

He grinned, the flash of even white teeth, knife-shimmeringly bright, quite disconcerting her. 'Oh, Rosalind,' he whispered, when she gave a small intake of breath. His lips were on hers, gentle and warm.

She shuddered the length of her body, her eyes closed to reality, savouring the last embrace she'd have. He took the glasses from her shaking hands one by one without lifting his mouth from hers and she heard them fall somewhere to the floor. And then he groaned in need, his lips skimming the surface of her skin all along her collarbone to her shoulder.

'Chance,' she said, trying to bring herself back from the world of dreams. 'Take the necklace. I don't want that kind of present——'

'You accepted the earrings,' he reminded her, his voice muffled in the depths of her hair and warming her scalp deliciously.

'I'd forgotten! They're still in the packet—somewhere in the drawer——' She broke off, her voice quivering.

He was chewing her earlobe and his tongue glided sensually around its curves. 'Perhaps you want another present instead. One you've been wanting a long time.'

Rosalind felt his hand draw down the sheet between their bodies and then he was sliding the necklace over her skin to lie on her breasts. She felt she couldn't breathe. His mouth trailed along the top curve of the emeralds in a sensual sweep and then beneath and the touch of his fingers lifted her breasts high to his mouth in immediate and condemning evidence of her desire.

'You do want me,' he whispered.

'You're making me feel cheap!' she moaned. 'You wine and dine me and you give me a good time and you give me jewellery... Do you think you can buy me?'

Chance lifted his dark head and kissed her passionately. 'No, I don't,' he said huskily. 'Don't misunderstand. We had a good evening. You seemed willing to continue it——'

'What? When? What did I say?' she demanded hotly, wishing her body would still down.

'Can't you read signs?' he chided. 'You don't know what you promised me out there, with your big blue eyes?'

'No, I don't,' she said miserably.

'Well, I do. And you're still sending blazing signals that are setting me alight,' he muttered, roughly pushing all the bedclothes aside and brutally exposing her nude body. Too proud to lose her dignity and grab the sheet from his hand, she lay there stiffly while her body seethed like the turbulent winds of a tornado inside.

'You're taking advantage of your physical strength,' she mumbled, her lips very dry. 'And you know I can't scream or Melanie will wake. Don't ruin everything, Chance. Let me leave this house without hating you.'

'If you're leaving,' he said, his eyes glittering, 'then I have to make love to you or I'll go crazy.'

'And I'll go crazy if you do,' she whispered.

'Really?' he drawled, running an exploratory finger down her body. It jerked spasmodically, offering itself to him, and he mocked her with his hard, merciless eyes. 'You make it all so much more exciting,' he said in admiration. 'You know just how far to go in refusing me to drive me wild with desire. So wild,' he growled, grabbing her shoulders, 'that I am barely in control of myself.'

'Tom,' she said, clutching frantically at anything that would stop him. 'He's——'

'Irrelevant,' he murmured. 'I told you, I don't care about your boyfriends, past or present. Only you and me. Don't you remember how it was for us?' he breathed urgently in her ear. 'When we made love the last time it was like nothing I've ever known. It can't be as good with him. Chemistry like that, the spontaneous combustion we achieved, only happens once.' He took her face in his hands and possessed her mouth as if he wanted to obliterate everything except the sensation of his lips, the masculine scents of his body, the feel of him pressing down on her and the soft growl of need in his throat. 'You're leaving for ever, Ros!' he muttered, almost in anger, his eyes fierce. 'Say goodbye with your body. End my obsession and let me get on with my life.'

Rosalind stared back at him numbly. This was like the last time when he'd left for Martinique. Once again they were about to part and he intended to say goodbye the only way he knew how where attractive women were concerned.

'I don't think you understand,' she whispered. 'We had a good time this evening, that's all we were doing. We came close to being friends——'

'*Friends*?' he snarled, pushing himself up and leaning menacingly over her. 'I'm not interested in being your friend, Rosalind. I want to be your lover. I want to leave you with a lasting memory of me.'

She felt hysterical laughter bubbling up inside her. He'd done that once! Oh, how thoroughly he'd done that... The laughter became uncontrollable. Chance caught her shoulders and shook her but it made no difference. She couldn't stop laughing, the tears streaming down her face.

'Stop it!' he ordered.

'C-c-c-can't!' she jerked.

'Dammit, Ros! You're hysterical.'

He slapped her, lightly yet sharply, judging what would bring her under control without pain. The shock sobered her immediately. Her hand went up to where he'd hit her, the flesh feeling hot and faintly stinging. She lay very still and tense, the whites of her eyes big and bright and accusing in the darkness.

'You hit me!' she whispered.

'You once hit me.'

She bridled. 'I'm a woman!'

'More than you know.' He accompanied his words with an insolent caress of her breast. Then his face hardened as if he contemplated something more malicious. 'A woman without mercy deserves none,' he muttered.

'What are you going to do to me?' she quavered.

She felt him begin to move over her and she squealed in terror, but then she realised he had kept going and his feet had hit the floor. There was a sound like a stifled curse.

'Do? Leave you to stew. I'm going to leave well alone. You can have one more day here,' he said in a savage rasp that seemed to be torn from his throat. 'Tell Melanie in the morning that you are leaving. If you stay any longer, I won't be responsible for your safety.'

His hand descended on her jaw and he held it in a grip of iron. His chest heaved in anger and frustration and she felt the energy pouring off him like a river in full spate. Chance's hot, harsh breath hissed from his bared teeth and she thought he was going to hit her again.

'You've ruined my lovely evening!' she mumbled
miserably.

'Damn you, Rosalind!' he growled. 'That's nothing
to what you've done to me.'

He grabbed the necklace from the sheets where it had
fallen and flung himself away. The door slammed behind
him and Rosalind lay in a cold sweat, her limbs trembling uncontrollably. It was a long time before she could
get up and bolt the door and the windows. Chance was
a mystery to her. Dangerous, passionate, contradictory.
Not good father material at all. And yet she was being
forced by circumstances to trust him with Melanie. She
was afraid for her child's well-being but she didn't see
how she could stay. Distracted, she picked up a novel
and read it from start to finish through the long, hot
darkness of the night without ever being aware of the
words.

Rosalind lay exhausted after breakfast in a heavily
fringed linen hammock slung between two massive evergreen oaks, gazing up into the tracery of branches and
trying to find the right way to tell Melanie that she was
leaving. And the minute she thought she'd composed
her speech she wondered if she should go after all.
Melanie's small hands were gently rocking the hammock
and she was reading a highly lurid adventure story to
Rosalind.

'Here's Daddy and Blanche,' Melanie said suddenly.
'He can hear the rest of my story. Hi, Pops,' she said
irreverently. 'Where did you have breakfast?'

'Honey, you don't ask grown men things like that!'
exclaimed Blanche, suppressing a giggle.

Rosalind scowled. It was perfectly clear where he'd
had breakfast. In bed. Blanche's. He looked relaxed and
very content with life whereas she was edgy and frustrated and resentful.

'Morning, sweetheart.' Chance kissed his daughter fondly. His face chilled. 'Rosalind.'

'Morning,' she said distantly. 'Morning, Blanche.'

'Hi. You two had a spat?' grinned Blanche. 'Atmosphere's awful chilly.'

'It'll be arctic if you make any more remarks like that,' said Chance irritably.

'You old bear! Ros...don't mind if I take Chance away?' cooed Blanche. 'We've got a few things to chew over.'

'Chew as much of him as you like,' said Rosalind magnanimously. 'Don't spit any bits my way, that's all I ask.'

'You two's always gettin' in a huddle 'n talkin',' accused Melanie.

'Neighbourly chats,' Blanche said smugly.

'Neighbours?' queried Rosalind in amazement, sitting up straighter. She frowned at the implications. Blanche wasn't a good influence on Melanie at all. And how many nights would Chance spend with Blanche next door, instead of moving into the house to be with his daughter?

'We could be changing that situation soon,' husked Blanche, lifting her big eyes to Chance. Rosalind's mouth tightened. 'Why, honey!' cried Blanche gaily. 'Looks like there's a row of pins in your mouth! I'd swear you were jealous, if I didn't know better.'

'Daddy's seen Ros naked,' announced Melanie slyly.

Rosalind blushed to the roots of her hair. 'Melanie, you know that was an accident. We were in bed and——'

'You were in *bed*?' cried Blanche, her mouth agape. 'Chance, honey, if you really want that "something special" you've been chasin' these last few months,' she cooed, the sugar in her voice barely hiding the bald threat, 'you'd better come back with me and be nice to me.' She strolled away, very sure of herself.

'Damn!' swore Chance. 'Women!' he muttered. And to Rosalind's fury he scowled at Blanche's swaying figure but followed her nevertheless.

'I'm going too,' said the fascinated Melanie. 'I want to know what they're doin'.'

'No!' cried Rosalind quickly. 'I'd rather see if your pony can jump that new fence your daddy made. That'll be much more fun.'

Neighbours, she thought, as Melanie danced around her happily on the way to the stables. She'd never imagined Blanche lived so close. Was that where he went when he said he was going to ease his frustration elsewhere? Her teeth dug into her lower lip. All the while Melanie proudly showed off her pony's prowess Rosalind tried not to imagine what Chance *was* doing, but it was hard, terribly hard.

He came back slowly, as if he was exhausted, some time after she and Melanie had returned to the hammock. Rosalind resolutely kept her eyes away from his and crossly cuddled Melanie, who was sprawled on her, listening to a story Rosalind was inventing.

'I thought we'd have a picnic,' he said casually.

'I'm a bit tired,' began Rosalind.

Melanie rolled over to frown at Rosalind, her face disappointed. 'Please,' she said unhappily. 'You can't spend today on your own. It's too lovely. And you'll be crazy about the riverbank.' She flung her arms around Rosalind and lay over her coaxingly, rocking them both from side to side.

Rosalind looked daggers at Chance and buried her face in Melanie's thick dark hair. 'Yes, my darling,' she said softly, unable to deny her anything today. 'We'll go together.'

Melanie whooped with joy in Rosalind's ear, rolled off and executed a few cartwheels. She began to run off, yelling that she'd arrange the food with Kate.

Chance leaned over her. 'You'll tell her that you're leaving. This must be your last outing at Sans Souci.'

She stared up at him miserably. He seemed to be deliberately tormenting her. 'I'm aware of that,' she said quietly.

'It's a fitting place, isn't it, Rosalind, the riverbank? Silent, unobserved, full of atmosphere. Melanie will be able to fish and you and I can lie back and doze in the shade of a garden parasol and talk about old times.'

His voice grew husky and it seemed to Rosalind that a hushed silence had descended on the sultry morning. 'Old times,' he said harshly. 'Remember those mint juleps on the balcony by Preservation Hall, with the sound of saxophones belting out hot jazz? That ride in the *calèche*, that little surrey with the fringe on top, when I kissed you for the first time...something like this——'

Rosalind started. Mesmerised by memories, she had let him come kissing-close. Yes. This was the kiss that had taken her by storm, she thought helplessly, as he pressed her body into the hammock. It was tender, gentle and as sweet as praline candy. She sighed. Chance was lightly kissing her fingers now, his eyes dark pools of treacherous promises.

'Stop that,' she said sharply. 'You're not with Blanche any longer.'

'Jealous?' he smirked infuriatingly.

'Don't be ridiculous.' Her mouth set stubbornly while she struggled with her curiosity about his beautiful neighbour.

'She wants me,' he confided.

'I can't think why,' she said with casual indifference. 'Will she get you?' she asked, hoping she wasn't revealing how keenly she awaited his reply.

He laughed softly and fingered the sweat-slicked curls on Rosalind's neck, his hands cool on her hot skin. 'You sound as if you care.'

'I do,' she said haughtily. 'Though not for the reason you imagine. To be honest, I think you're probably well suited, but she'd ruin Melanie,' she said, her eyes stormy. 'I'm sure you wouldn't want that.'

'I'm working on the solution to the problem,' he said enigmatically and he left her to see to the picnic while Rosalind remained in the hammock and spent her time worrying about her daughter's future. With Blanche next door, ready to pounce on Chance and corrupt Melanie, the situation was looking bleaker by the minute.

'We done all Cajun an' Creole food. Come on,' urged Melanie, tugging at the side of the hammock impatiently.

Rosalind felt herself falling and tumbled out into Chance's arms. For a wonderful, adrenalin-flowing moment, their cotton-clad bodies were glued together in an intimate embrace and she was locking startled, longing eyes with his. And then he had firmly set her apart.

'Promising start,' he said lazily. 'I must encourage my daughter to throw you off balance more often.'

'Isn't she nice to cuddle, Daddy?' grinned Melanie.

'Sumptuous.'

'What's that mean?'

'Soft and cushiony, warm, gloriously luxurious...'

She heard no more of his outrageous explanation. She had glared and let her hair flow forwards to hide her face from him, then walked smartly on. Every touch, every look only made her feel more unhappy.

He and Melanie followed and in a moment a small hand crept into hers. 'Sumshus,' smiled Melanie and Rosalind couldn't help but laugh reluctantly.

They set off towards the river, through the groves of magnolias and pink-flowered crape myrtle and then into the parkland that surrounded the house. In the heat of the sun, Rosalind put her wide-brimmed hat on her head and was able to keep Chance out of her eye-line.

He looked too handsome for any woman's good. The soft cream shirt and dove-grey cotton jeans were designer-cut for an Adonis and he fitted them perfectly. His dark sunglasses would have given him an air of mystery if it weren't for the permanent grin on his face, and she tried not to wish that it was her hand he was holding, instead of just Melanie's.

The little girl bounced along, singing and executing a few dance-steps. Rosalind felt a tug of great pride.

'Sweetheart, you choose our base camp,' suggested Chance. Melanie rushed off excitedly.

'You've made her very happy,' said Rosalind, an inner warmth flooding her face with radiance.

'I love her to pieces.'

'You won't let Blanche get her hands on her, will you?' she asked anxiously.

'That woman belongs in one place only,' he answered with amusement. 'And that certainly isn't my daughter's life.'

'I'm very relieved.' She pushed down her resentment that Blanche would soon have full reign in Chance's bed.

'You can go with a clear conscience, can't you?' he said lightly.

And she nodded. Almost a clear conscience, she thought. He surely was too fond of Melanie to do anything that would be bad for her. But he was giving all his undivided attention to Melanie at the moment. Would he keep it up in the future?

Walking beside Chance in the sunshine, the oppressive heat stilling even the bees, Rosalind gradually became aware of the tension between them both. It crackled in the air, linking their bodies and surrounding her in a highly charged electric field so that every part of her was sensitised to Chance's smallest movements.

The way his long legs shifted in the summer-weight jeans, betraying the muscles beneath. The way his hands hung easily at his sides, the strong forearms shapely and infinitely touchable. The unconscious swagger of the broad shoulders, his serious, thoughtful gaze ahead as if he were in another world, not this.

They reached the place Melanie had chosen and let her arrange the huge rug. Rosalind sank down beneath the delicate mimosa with a satisfied sigh. 'Perfect,' she said softly, hugging Melanie. 'Paradise.'

'I'm fishin'. You comin'?' Melanie grinned happily at them both, full of hope and childish eagerness.

'I'll come,' said Chance huskily. 'Are you staying here, Rosalind?' She nodded, her eyes devouring his love-softened face.

'We go off to do things and you stay home. Jus' like mommies and daddies,' said Melanie.

Rosalind met Chance's amused eyes and resolutely let that one go. Time enough for her to teach Melanie that women didn't all stay at home—and, if they did, that they were still equal ... She bit her lip. No. There was no time. A few hours left, that was all.

She watched them go as if watching her life vanish. Alone, she sat surrounded in the humming heat, so intense and sultry that it almost throbbed. She let the morning slip by, her mind going over the richly fulfilling hours she'd spent with Melanie. And Chance.

The love in his eyes when he read the bedtime story. His patience in teaching his daughter tennis strokes. The way he pitched in and cleared up after a session of cooking crawfish Creole.

It was the small things that had cemented her love for Chance—the way he watched his daughter as she sprawled on the floor, reading, and leant forwards to touch her hair so lightly that she was unaware of the caress. The way he smiled to himself when he carefully moved some of Melanie's cuddly toys when she was asleep, so that she had room to sleep.

She knew she'd never love as deeply as she did now, not ever. But she'd had more brief yet potent joy than many women had in a lifetime. The trouble was that it had been packed into tiny, intense moments and it was to be a short-lived happiness.

Wistfully she followed the progress of the huge, gaudy dragonflies blithely flitting over the dazzling sheet of water in front of her, dipping frenziedly to the elephant's ear plants and water hyacinth as if life was short and should be filled with pleasure.

An orange butterfly with black veins fluttered to her knee and she smiled, then became aware that she was being watched.

'It's a Monarch butterfly,' Chance said, looking up at the sky, which had become sprinkled with their fluttering wings. His face became rapt as he gazed at the butterfly which had just alighted on his arm. 'They use the Mississippi as their highway to the Mexican gulf. Then they fly on to Venezuela,' he said gently. 'These are a bit early this year. Probably the advance party. Seems as if everyone's leaving,' he added lightly.

'Yes,' she mumbled.

'Melanie's carrying on for a while and then she's coming in for a refuel.' With the butterflies flocking around his head, he sat down in front of her, his eyes hidden behind the sunglasses. 'When will you tell her?' he asked in a low, throaty voice.

'After the picnic. I don't want to spoil her day,' she said as steadily as she could.

His hand touched her shoulder in a hesitant touch. 'I'm afraid it will.'

'We all have to learn sorrow,' she said shakily. 'I wish I didn't have to make Melly unhappy, though.'

He was silent for a while, morosely tearing up blades of grass. 'Maybe she's young enough not to care,' he said, without conviction. 'She shouldn't mind too much. After all, she's only known you for a short while.'

'That's right. To her, I'm nothing more than a godmother who's mislaid her wand,' Rosalind said with a light laugh to hide her unhappiness.

'That's how you *should* be,' he agreed quietly. 'But you've given her a depth of love that goes far beyond the casual fondness of someone with no blood-link.'

She felt the panic rising within her, the racing of her pulses, and sought hastily to allay his suspicions. 'Girls of that age have crushes. They often idolise their teachers, for instance,' she said dismissively. 'I came at a vulnerable time for her.'

'Yet,' he mused, 'I wonder how different it would have been if you'd come to Martinique with me as you'd wanted, instead of Annie?'

She flinched. He would have known she was pregnant, for a start, she thought bitterly. 'Don't play that "if only" game,' she said shakily.

'If we'd married,' he said, ruthlessly ignoring her, 'I think we would have got on well together. I don't believe we would have had these problems with Melanie. We should have married, Rosalind.'

'Please, Chance——'

'You know,' he went on remorselessly, 'that kiddie should have been ours.'

'Oh!' she mouthed on an intake of pained breath. The brim of her hat hid her wounded eyes; a brush of her hand over her ribs, as if to remove an insect, hid the sudden collapse of her lungs. 'Annie did her best——' she began in a half-gasp.

'It wasn't ever good enough.' Chance stared into the distance where the Mississippi curved in a shimmering silver sheet. 'She never loved Melanie. Not the way you seem to. She had to force herself to act like a normal mother. I watched her try and fail and it baffled me.'

'Oh, no!' groaned Rosalind, unable to bear what he was saying. Annie had lied to her about the good times.

'You see?' he frowned, his finger gently gliding over the inner satin of her forearm. 'You can't understand that behaviour in a woman. You must have a natural mothering instinct.'

'Dear heaven!' she whispered.

His hand turned her face to him and thoughtfully his thumb rubbed at the teardrops trickling down her face. 'You don't want to go,' he whispered.

'Well, I——' She drew in a long, shuddering breath.

'Because of Melanie or me?' he asked huskily.

Trapped, Rosalind stared dumbly at him. If she protested that it was Melanie too fiercely then he'd wonder why. That would leave him as the reason. In fact it was both, and New Orleans, and Sans Souci...the broad sweep of his forehead, the way his jaw set with determination, the strong hands...Melanie's spiky little lashes after her bath, the gurgle of joy when she came into Rosalind in the mornings, her sweet, sleepy face...the cool breeze on the bayou and the sultry summer nights, the rustle of the long meadow grass beyond the living oaks. These things were the whole world to her.

'I love the deep south,' she said quietly.

'With its slow, steamy passions.'

She felt numb. 'There are times,' she said, her voice constricted in her throat, 'when I could cheerfully hit you.'

He dabbed with his handkerchief at her tear-sprinkled face. 'There are times, Rosalind, when I'd welcome that, if it meant you'd touch me,' he said softly.

The tension stretched between them. 'Why do we always want what we can't have?' she asked bleakly.

'Because we're driven,' he answered huskily. 'Perhaps to repeat a well-remembered happiness. Perhaps because we know that anything hard-won is worth cherishing.'

She tilted her head back, too choked to speak, watching the dainty mimosa leaves trembling in the light breeze. Chance's face was very close to hers now and her skin tingled with his nearness.

'I'll always remember it here,' she said with a gentle passion.

'And me?'

Her head slowly lowered and she stared into the mid-distance, smiling faintly. 'You're unforgettable,' she told him drily.

He laughed deep in his throat and Rosalind wondered if all women in love found their lover's every breath and gesture a source of unbearable longing as she did. The impulse to fling her arms around him was very strong. It was only a sense of self-preservation that kept her from doing so.

'This is where you belong. You always have. Here in Louisiana. On my land, in my arms.'

Her eyes slanted to his and the longing in his expression made her shake her head in futile denial that he was right. 'No. No, no, no,' she whispered.

His hand tenderly stroked her cheek and imperceptibly she moved her face into the caress, aware of the breeze catching her hair and lifting it from her neck. Or was that Chance's touch again? She closed her eyes and let out a soft sigh.

'We can't resist it for long, can we?' he marvelled in a low, hungry growl that vibrated deep into her body. She licked her dry lips and felt the touch of his tongue there.

Her eyes shot open then. She was shaken by the soft, caressing look he was giving her, and half closed her lids in drowsy near-surrender. 'Resist what?' she mumbled, confused.

'That deep, carnal desire of yours.'

He kissed her and in the slow, languorous heat she felt she had no energy or will-power to stop him. He laid her back gently on the rug, kissing away her tears while the midday heat sapped her strength and any desire to resist.

For a while he just held her then, in his arms, content it seemed merely to be with her. And she fought her common sense and her conscience all the way, resenting the fact that she knew perfectly well she ought to extricate herself from his embrace.

But she'd be a long time alone, soon. There would be no one to love, or to love her—not as she loved Chance. A small shudder ran through her and she clung tightly to him, burying her face in his chest while his strong arms enclosed her as if he never wanted to let her go.

'I don't know why you're leaving,' he husked into her small ear. He accompanied his words with kisses, then turned her head so that he could kiss her other ear too. Her mouth was being plundered. Beautifully.

'You don't know how to be faithful,' she said sadly.

His chest expanded with his indrawn breath and he slowly drew his arms from her and sat up. Rosalind felt bereft. She stared mournfully at his broad back, wishing he'd hold her again and they could pretend they were both in love.

There came the sound of singing and his head turned to where Melanie skipped along happily as if she hadn't a care in the world. His eyes flicked to Rosalind, and he frowned at her hungry, devouring stare as she tried to fix every inch of her daughter on her brain to hold in her memory.

'What would you do to preserve Melanie's happiness?' he asked, his voice thin with strain.

Rosalind shot him a wary glance. 'Why do you ask?' she asked suspiciously.

'Answer the damn question!' he said softly.

'Depends,' she dissembled.

'Hmm.'

To escape Chance's hypnotic eyes, she ran to Melanie and took some of the Spanish moss from her, joining in a silly dance, whirling around with it and collapsing with giggles in a heap, the two of them weak with laughter.

But Chance wasn't laughing this time. Instead, there was a determined look about his face that brought a chill of fear into Rosalind's body. He was planning something. She hoped nervously that it wasn't another of his emotionally explosive goodbye gifts.

All through lunch, he was distant and preoccupied, even during the lazy afternoon when he took them up-river in the *pirogue*—the swamp-boat—to count alligators.

'Come and climb trees with me, Daddy,' demanded Melanie, as they made their way back home past the renovated plank houses, raised from the ground on brick pillars. Once they'd been the slave quarters. Now they housed the families of the people who worked for Chance.

'Please,' he prompted.

'Sorry. Please?' his daughter asked more humbly. 'Show me how to go high,' she coaxed.

'Take care, sweetheart,' said Rosalind anxiously. 'Chance, see she doesn't take risks——'

'One tree only,' he told the demure Melanie. 'It'll be dark soon.'

'I'll wait on the stoop of this house; I'm sure no one will mind,' said Rosalind. 'Don't be long—and ... take care.'

She worried about the set of Chance's shoulders and the knot of muscles that she'd seen tensing across his back. He was on the edge and his temper seemed to be simmering close beneath the surface, ready to erupt. Her own nerves were so jittery that she couldn't keep still, with the sense of foreboding growing greater every minute.

Rosalind rose, clutching the veranda rail. When they came back, nearly half an hour later, Melanie was tagging behind Chance reluctantly, scuffing her feet and hanging her head. Closer to, Rosalind cold see that both of them were in a filthy mood.

'Something wrong?' she asked quietly. 'Oh, Melanie!' she cried in alarm, seeing where tears had washed a clean path through her grubby face. She knelt down on the coarse grass and Melanie ran into Rosalind's embrace.

'Ouch!' she winced, drawing back, her face pained.

'Darling, your bruises!' Rosalind froze in the act of examining the marks on Melanie's small brown arms. Slowly her eyes lifted to Chance who was standing like a threatening thundercloud, his hands clenching and unclenching as if he wanted to hit someone. 'What happened?' whispered Rosalind. Her arms went around the bruised child, and she stared accusingly at Chance.

'He hurt me!' wailed Melanie, slanting her eyes at Rosalind to see her reaction.

He went chalk-white. 'Melly! How can you say that?' he growled. 'It was an accident——'

'You did hurt me, you did!'

Rosalind stroked the child's forehead gently. 'We'll go and get you cleaned up and find something for those bruises,' she said firmly, deciding the only way to deal with this was by taking one step at a time.

With Melanie sniffing unhappily beside her, she walked back to the house, her whole body trembling with anger. If he had been careless and caused her daughter's accident, she'd take him apart with her bare hands.

'Tell him to go,' pouted Melanie, when Chance hovered like a brooding dark shadow in the doorway of the pretty pink bedroom. Her eyes fluttered at Rosalind. 'I want you. I don't want Daddy,' she said plaintively.

'You've learnt your lesson well,' muttered Chance, his hands thrust aggressively in his pockets and meeting Melanie's sulky glare with one of his own.

Rosalind turned around in the doorway of the en-suite bathroom and flinched at the hurt in his eyes. 'What lesson have you been teaching my...' Her eyes flickered. 'My goddaughter?' she demanded haughtily, recovering from the error.

'Not me! I'm not the teacher! If you can't see it, you're blind,' he growled, watching her gently slide Melanie's dress over her head. 'Don't you recognise the crude imitation of Blanche's coaxing ways?'

'Well, I don't know as much about Blanche's coaxing ways as you apparently do,' said Rosalind savagely, wincing at the sight of the bruises on Melanie's arms. 'How did this happen?' she raged at Chance. He opened his mouth but Melanie sniffed and spoke first.

'He was cross,' she whined.

'Sweet heaven!' he said grimly. 'I've a good mind to——'

'You come one step nearer, Chance Decatur, and I'll show you what real fighting dirty is like,' seethed Rosalind, her eyes blazing blue fire.

'Sheath your claws. You're like a hell-cat defending her young,' he growled. Rosalind stiffened in alarm, but he was too angry to notice anyone but himself. 'She fell out of the tree and I caught her on the way down,' he said tightly.

Rosalind looked at Melanie enquiringly. She was staring at her father, her eyes huge, tears rolling down her cheeks. But she didn't confirm his story.

'You don't understand, Daddy,' she wailed. 'You don't see why and I—I can't bear it!'

'No. I don't see!' gritted Chance through his clenched teeth.

Rosalind heard him leave. Steeling her heart to his anguish, she cleaned the distressed Melanie up, tucked her up in bed and gave her a drink of milk. If Chance found it hard to bear when his daughter rejected him, then he should be more careful in the first place, she thought angrily.

Melanie hugged her tightly. 'Daddy said you were going away. You're not, are you? You wouldn't leave me alone.'

Rosalind shut her eyes and groaned. He'd roughly blurted out what she'd meant to say gently in a well-rehearsed explanation. 'Oh, Melly——'

'Don't go away,' sobbed her daughter brokenly. 'I can't bear it. No one stays with me. I love you, Ros.'

'Sweetheart——'

Rosalind felt a lump come into her throat. Her child, her little girl, had been torn this way and that, dragged from her real mother's arms by 'concerned' welfare officers. She'd been farmed out to Annie who couldn't love her because she was consumed with guilt at deceiving her husband. She'd witnessed the quarrels which had led to divorce. Then she'd been tossed from one nanny to another till she could trust no one to remain with her permanently.

Rosalind sat in her own private hell, incapable of moving or of stopping the silent tears from pouring down her face. Then the tears were so blinding that she could see nothing.

'Ros,' howled Melanie. 'Ros, don't cry! I love you; don't cry, don't!'

The two of them sobbed together. 'Darling, it's all right,' sniffed Rosalind. 'It's really fine. I'm glad you love me. I love you too.'

''Snice,' said Melanie shakily.

Rosalind willed herself to stop exchanging affection with her daughter because she knew she was on the brink of confessing.

Those wonderful words. *I am your mother.*

She longed to say them more than anything in the world. She gave a juddering sob and bit her lip hard. There was no way that she could abandon her child.

'I'm not going away. Not now. I couldn't.'

That seemed to calm Melanie. After making sure she was sleeping, Rosalind went to the up-river drawing-room to have a word with Chance. Or several.

The room was softly lit by candles and gas-lamps, the scent of roses heavily in the air. Rosalind put a hand on one of the fine rosewood buttonback chairs to steady her trembling legs while Chance paced up and down in front of the marbled fireplace, his dark, grim profile repeatedly appearing in the gilt-framed French mirror above.

She'd taken a decision she might regret, but she'd never rest if she returned to England and left Melanie without proper supervision. Chance was obviously not to be trusted.

'What happened?' asked Rosalind, coming straight to the point.

'We had a row——'

'You what?' she cried, shocked.

'Let me explain! You know *nothing*!' he yelled. 'We were halfway up a tree. High up. She was in my arms and we were talking like old friends. It seemed the best time to tell her you were going because she told me she loved me and I thought she could turn to me for comfort. God, Ros, how do you think I feel about what's happened? Don't you know I'd fall into a vat of boiling oil for her?' he asked hoarsely.

'How did she get bruised?' asked Rosalind coldly. 'You lost your temper?'

'*No*! Falling out of the tree.' He pushed a hand through his hair distractedly. 'I reached out and I grabbed her. I stopped her from falling...'

He closed his eyes and he couldn't continue for a while, walking to the window to open it and flinging back the jalousies with an almighty crash. Rosalind saw him take in several deep breaths and wondered if he'd been as badly affected by Melanie's near-brush with death as it seemed.

When he turned, his face was quite composed. 'I had one hand around her arm, the other around her leg,' he continued in a flat, hard tone. 'That's how she got the bruises. If I hadn't grabbed her hard enough, her weight would have driven her through my hands.'

'Then if you saved her life, why was she so angry with you?' asked Rosalind quietly.

Chance slammed his fist into his palm, the control breaking instantly. 'She thinks I've sent you away!' he raged.

'She's right. Your behaviour made it impossible for me to stay,' said Rosalind with chilling ruthlessness.

He paused in an attempt to gather himself together. 'I need a drink,' he muttered. 'You?' She shook her head and he poured out a double slug of bourbon then resumed his pacing, glass cradled in his hand.

'However, I'm staying,' she told him in a hard, flat tone.

His drink slopped. 'What?'

'I have to, don't I?' she said bitterly. 'I promised Annie I'd take care of Melly till I wasn't needed. By endangering Melly's life, you've made me realise it would be fatal for me to let you near that child unless I'm there too. Besides, you've ruined everything we've done to bring you two together. She feels angry and betrayed by you. I'll have to start all over again. That's all I have to say. Do you have any more excuses or explanations you want to make?'

His back was to her, but his shoulders were lifted high in unexploded anger. 'No. None.'

'Then keep your distance from me,' she said scathingly. 'Because I despise any man who is so cavalier with a child's life and because there'll be all hell let loose if you cause that kiddie any harm, innocently or not. And that goes for me, too, though in my case I doubt anything you plan for me would be innocent. I hope your conscience will allow you to sleep. If it were me, I'd need a bottle of pills to settle me down. Goodnight.'

She swept out and behind her she heard an ornament crash on the grate. Let him take his rage out on objects, she thought in contempt, even if they were French porcelain.

He drove away early the next morning, and, to Rosalind's astonishment, Melanie was very upset. She cried so continuously, repeating over and over that her daddy didn't understand, that Rosalind was forced to ring Chance's office.

'Chance Decatur, please,' she snapped at his secretary.

'Who's calling him?'

'Just tell him that Melanie won't stop crying.' Rosalind banged down the phone, too distraught with the screaming to explain any more.

'Excuse me, Miss Ros'lin'?'

'Oh, Kate!' Rosalind smiled ruefully. 'Melanie's in good voice today.'

'Mr Chance, he's with Miss Blanche,' said Kate, vigorously dusting the mahogany table. She moved on and attacked a Victorian sideboard. 'You want her number?'

'Please,' sighed Rosalind, hearing the sounds of hysterical sobs from above. Hastily, wanting to comfort Melanie, she rang and waited for a long—too long— time before Blanche answered. 'Tell Chance that Melanie's very upset,' said Rosalind stiffly.

'Oh, it's you,' said Blanche rudely. 'We were just getting started. You sure picked a bad time to call. Can't it wait?'

'No! And if you don't tell him right now I'm coming over, and I don't care if he's naked and in bed with you— I'll drag him out and make him see that he has to do something about his daughter!' yelled Rosalind. The phone smashed into its cradle and Kate gave what sounded suspiciously like a pleased chuckle.

'Three for lunch, Miss Ros'lin'?' she asked innocently.

'If I have my way,' Rosalind muttered viciously, 'we'll be boiling Mr Chance Decatur and eating him half alive.'

'With Miss Blanche for dessert?' grinned Kate.

Rosalind laughed. 'Yes! That'd be perfect!'

She felt a little less tense now that she'd shared her frustrated anger with someone. She was really very fond of Kate. Like virtually everyone else on the plantation, Kate had been with Chance since he had first taken over from his parents. He seemed, oddly, to inspire loyalty in his staff and they all spoke of him with genuine affection. It was something she'd never understood.

Chance came and went straight up to his daughter, the tears stopping almost immediately. It was a long time till he came down again. He strolled nonchalantly towards her and she found herself trapped in a corner. He put a hand on either side of the wall, making a cage with his body.

She licked her lips and his eyes kindled.

'Do you do that deliberately, or is it a reflex action?' he asked softly.

'I do it because my lips are dry. In the heat,' she said sullenly.

'Well, it sure makes my guts twist for you.'

Her eyes widened. He'd moved even closer, his breath hot and heavy on her face, and she wanted to lift her head so that it whispered on her mouth, ebbing and flowing tantalisingly.

His mouth seemed to have found her ear and he laughed at her shuddering response to the slick of his tongue around the soft skin behind it. She groaned. He was savaging her throat with a thoroughness that left her without any sense in her head at all.

'Oh,' she whispered, her head tipping back in pleasure.

'God, you're responsive.'

'You were at Blanche's,' she said, wondering why her voice sounded as if a frog had jumped into her throat.

'So?'

'For what?' she grated, the jealousy eating away inside her.

'A little bit of southern comfort,' he drawled. She flinched. He smiled. And strolled out.

Rosalind buried her face in the voluminous drapes of the bed curtains. It shamed and horrified her that she didn't want him to go to Blanche to ease his male needs. She wanted him to come to *her*.

'I love him,' she whispered. 'I hate him. I hate and love him and I want to go home and live like a nun for the rest of my life in peace.'

CHAPTER SIX

'A WORD with you.'

Rosalind, exhausted from yet another energetic day, glanced up at Chance's imperious command and saw him leaning out of his study window. 'I'm too tired to traipse after you to your study,' she called back to him irritably. 'Talk to me here.'

He came out on to the gallery where she was lazing after dinner on the big rattan sofa, listening to the sounds of the soft, warm night, her head lifted to catch any breezes that came off the river.

'Is Melanie asleep?' he asked with a frown.

'Solid. You tired her out with that ride across the fields and then that water fight.'

She tried not to let him know by any hint of pleasure in her voice how much she'd enjoyed those, too. Odd, how Chance had behaved like an angel for the past week.

Father and child had been as close as old buddies and the little girl had gone out of her way to be affectionate towards him. If Rosalind hadn't seen the grazes and bruises on Melly's body, she would have suspected that the whole thing had been invented to persuade her to stay.

Chance pulled a chair close by her and sat down heavily in it. 'We've got trouble. Annie's done a bunk,' he said flatly.

'Oh, no! From the clinic? But she needs to continue her treatment!' she cried. Chance shrugged. 'Where's she gone? Is she on her way here?'

'No,' he answered in an irritable growl. 'She's cashed in all the bonds I put in her name as security. She has enough money to go anywhere and do anything she wants. I'm trying to trace her but it's a bit like looking for a needle in a haystack unless she contacts me.'

'Why would she do this?' asked Rosalind, bewildered.

He stared down at his big square fists broodingly as if he wished he could use them to alleviate his pent-up anger. 'Self-preservation. But . . . how can she abandon her own child?'

Rosalind flinched. 'You don't know she has for sure——' she began.

'Yes, I do!' His glittering eyes flashed up to lock with her startled blue ones. 'She left a note asking me to take care of Melanie in future.'

'She wouldn't do that,' said Rosalind hotly. 'She'd ask me first——'

'Why?' he demanded belligerently. 'Why should she ask you?' Rosalind stared at him silently, incapable of telling him. 'She did once. You told her there was no room in your life for my child. You made it quite plain that she would be a nuisance.'

'Oh. Yes. So I did.' Rosalind thought for a moment. 'She'll be back——'

'No. I think you should speak to the psychologist.' He looked at her from under the thick fringe of lashes. 'You see, he knows all about Annie.'

Her eyes widened. 'All?' she asked nervously, wondering if her secret was out.

'Sure. We've all known that there was only one path she could take if she was to recover. She told us——'

'What? What?' Rosalind demanded in agitation. Her heart hammered in her ribcage. She feared a confession from Annie. If anyone should tell Chance it must be her. But how he'd react when he learnt of the lies and the deceit she had no idea.

'She never wanted to live a lie again,' he said quietly.

'A lie!' she breathed. This was it. The moment she'd dreaded.

'She didn't want to return here and act as Melanie's mother,' he said, his eyes boring into Rosalind's.

She fought for calm. 'What can she mean, "act"?' she asked casually, her voice suddenly a few tones higher than normal.

'The experts seem to think that Melly is the cause of her problem,' said Chance. 'I know that is so. And why.'

The air seemed to thicken suddenly. Too agitated to stay seated, Rosalind jumped up and went to lean over the wooden balustrade, as if fascinated by the softly lit garden and its tropical night scents. 'Chance...' Her voice disappeared into a croaking whisper.

'Guilt,' he said softly.

She whirled around. 'What?'

'Annie's been guilty because she never could love Melanie, no matter how hard she tried,' he said. 'I imagine it's something to do with her loveless background—though yours didn't affect you that way. Odd, how personalities can be so different.'

Rosalind's body crumpled from relief and she forced herself to walk normally to the chair where she could hide her shaking legs. 'I see. Now what?' she said, worried.

He spread his hands in defeat. 'I have to accept the situation. But she's left me with one hell of a problem.'

Rosalind didn't know what to say to make things easier for him. 'Poor Melanie,' she muttered.

Chance nodded, seeming less concerned than he should in the circumstances. His eyes met hers in a calculating way. 'She needs friends. Company. I think I'll send her away to boarding-school——'

'Oh, no! You can't do that!' objected Rosalind. 'She can't be parted from her—her mother and father all in one go; she'll think you've all rejected her. Think what kind of a life she's had! Sending her away will hurt her dreadfully,' she said with passion.

'You mean she'll feel rejected?' he suggested. 'You're right. I can spent time with her mornings and evenings, but what happens in between? I work all day. I can't close down my business and sack all my employees so I can stay at home,' he said earnestly.

'Of course not,' frowned Rosalind.

'I suppose Kate could bring Melly up,' he mused. 'Though it would be hard for her to learn the things she'll need to know as a Decatur heiress.'

'A governess?' suggested Rosalind hesitantly.

'Too stern, don't you think? I need someone who can cuddle her and love her. A governess would need to be a schizophrenic to manage to be both tutor and mother.' He heaved a huge sigh. 'It looks as if the au pairs——'

'No!' said Rosalind sharply. 'I don't want that.'

He turned his dark eyes on her. 'Don't you?' he enquired silkily. 'What do you want? You're her godmother. You should have a say in what happens to her.'

She took a long, deep breath. If Melanie was that much of a nuisance to him... 'There's one possibility. We both agree she needs someone around she knows and loves. I—I could take her back to England with me and bring her up if you like,' she said in a strained voice.

'You?' he said incredulously.

'I'm her godmother, I love her,' she defended.

'Good grief, Ros, so do I—and I'm her father! I'm not letting her go!' he said in amazement.

'You really want her?' asked Rosalind tremulously. So did she, desperately, but she could never tell him how much.

'Of course I do! But I can't see how I'd be allowed to have custody of her—even in Annie's absence,' he frowned. 'My track record isn't very convincing. And if I apply to the courts for a chance of access, then my prison sentence will be public knowledge. That could damage my business immeasurably.'

'What are we to do?' despaired Rosalind.

He took her hands in his and clasped them in sympathy. 'It's a difficult one,' he said slowly. Then his forehead cleared. 'Unless...unless I was married, and married fast, before the authorities take her away from me.'

Rosalind's heart raced. 'Married?' she cried, aghast. 'Another loveless relationship——'

'Well, not entirely,' he said innocently. 'Blanche is crazy about me——'

'*No!*' Fiercely she snatched her hands away to grab Chance's arms and gave him a little shake. 'You couldn't allow that woman to be Melanie's stepmother!'

Chance looked a little bemused. 'No. Perhaps not. To overcome my disreputable reputation, my wife would have to be a decent woman who has Melanie's interests at heart. Some hopes.' He sighed again and gloomily stared out at the dark magnolias. 'Who do I know like that?'

There was a long pause with only the cicadas and the whirring fans above breaking the silence, and slowly, very slowly, Rosalind's head lifted.

'You could marry me,' she blurted out, and then blinked at her own temerity. What had she said?

'You? No.' Chance shook his head. 'Out of the question.'

She bridled. 'I'm no worse than Blanche La Salle!' she said crossly.

His lazy gaze wandered over her face and body. 'You've got better legs,' he said condescendingly, as if that was all. 'But Blanche could put up a good show of adoring me,' he continued quietly. 'You said yourself I shouldn't involve myself in a loveless marriage.'

'I love Melanie,' she said huskily.

'It's not enough,' he replied bluntly. 'You have to be wild about me too.'

Her lashes fluttered at the darkness of his eyes. Like a Louisiana summer day, there was a storm brewing behind that sultriness. Her mouth was dry. She both wanted and dreaded marriage to him.

'I could pretend. When we're together as a family, we get on well, we have fun.'

Chance's smile broadened until it gleamed white and mocking in the half-darkness. 'You said you didn't want permanent motherhood.'

'I've changed my mind.'

'Is that true? Or is it that you find you don't want to tear yourself away from a life of luxury?' he asked cynically.

She glared, but knew she had to let him think that. It gave her a good reason to be so determined to stay at Sans Souci that she'd even propose marriage. Her body flooded with embarrassment that she'd done such a thing and she saw his amusement at her pinkened face.

'I like the life here,' she said defiantly. 'So do you. Is that a crime?'

'A love of the good things in life isn't enough. We must have that added ingredient,' he said in his deep, seductive voice. 'Sex might do it.' His hand lifted in a brief but arousing touch of her extended leg and she quivered. 'Mmm. Maybe,' he mused. 'If you satisfied me in bed——'

'No. That's not necessary,' she said hastily. 'We can be friends.'

'Friends.' He seemed to consider the idea, an amused curl to his upper lip.

'It would work; I know it would,' she said earnestly.

'Only if the sex is good,' he drawled. He continued to smile at her steadily and she racked her brains for a way, any other way, to safeguard Melanie's future, but could come up with nothing less drastic. 'I want something in return.'

'You'd have a mother for your child. What more do you want?' she glared.

'A wife. In every sense. At my dinner table, at my side when I entertain, beneath me when I go to bed— or in any other position we dream up for our own amusement,' he murmured.

She gulped. 'I was thinking of a platonic arrangement,' she croaked. 'Businesslike.'

He chuckled. 'Forget it. I realise now that Melanie's future depends partly on the fact that she lives in a secure environment—and that means a father who is not the subject of idle gossip. Isn't that true?'

'I don't see what you're getting at,' she frowned.

'Simple, sweetheart. If you don't sleep with me, I'll need to go elsewhere. I can't go without sex, remember. I lust after women. Marry me and I'll be faithful to you forever, but only if I'm totally satisfied in bed. You'd have to work hard for your share of the Decatur name and fortune.' His eyes glittered with enjoyment at her discomfort. 'I'd make you earn what you want to take without effort,' he growled, the undercurrent of sensuality making her whole body tremble. 'Sex would be the foundation of our marriage. And I'd want you to play the whore whenever I snapped my fingers.'

'I—I wouldn't know how,' she said in a cracked voice.

'I'll teach you,' he said callously. He reached out and touched her tremulous mouth. 'It will be very enjoyable,' he added, his voice thickening with desire. 'Having you where I want you, in my power. My own personal possession, available whenever the need takes me.'

'That's no basis for a stable marriage,' she mumbled, her breath short and fast from the dangerous excitement simmering inside her. To be in his bed, night after night, in his arms... She shivered, afraid of a future under his arrogant domination.

'Then it'll have to be Blanche after all. Beggars can't be choosers,' he said with regret, moving rapidly down the steps. 'No time like the present. For Melanie's sake, I must make my move now. I'll go to her now and ask.'

'No!' She drove her teeth into her lower lip. He'd stopped halfway down and was waiting, motionless. He seemed to be expecting her to continue speaking but she couldn't. So he went on again and began to stroll along Oak Alley.

Rosalind brought her fist to her mouth to stifle a moan of despair. Her child's happiness lay in the balance. She knew what he wanted and she had no choice at all but to humble herself and beg for him.

Hating him for causing her to demean herself so abjectly, she ran lightly down to the path.

'Chance! Stop!' He took no notice and she gritted her teeth, kicking off her shoes and picking up her skirts so that she could run faster to catch up with his rapidly increasing strides.

At last she caught his arm and turned him around, there in the darkness, her breathing ragged, her heart thudding violently.

'You've got to listen to me!' she implored. 'I hate you, I loathe you and despise you, but I love Melanie more than all of that and you must let me marry you! There'll be nothing wrong with what we do in bed. In fact,' she said, defiantly tossing up her head, 'you'll probably find it titillating to have a partner who is reluctantly willing, who you can coax into submission against her better judgement.'

'You are proposing?' he murmured, lights dancing in his eyes.

'Proposing?' She laughed harshly. 'I'm abasing myself!' she grated. 'I'm begging you. I'm crawling the length of Oak Alley—just as you wanted. I'll be obliging in bed for you. Whenever and however you want. I'll crawl and crawl and crawl again. That's what you've always wanted, isn't it?'

'Sounds satisfactory,' he said laconically.

She felt consumed with anger at his triumphant expression, a red mist dancing in front of her eyes. 'Have what you want of my body till you're sated,' she seethed. 'But don't ever imagine you'll have my heart or my respect, because I will never give you those, not as long as I live.'

'Such passion,' he mocked. 'I've never had a better offer. Sex without strings. No heart involved.'

'Well?' she demanded vehemently.

'How do I know you mean this?' he asked suspiciously. 'You could be only saying this to get your hands on my money.'

'How can you doubt my word?' she raged.

He shrugged. 'Well, you haven't exactly put yourself about for me. I need proof——'

Furious, her eyes lashing with scorn, she ripped open his jacket and slid her hands up his chest. Standing on tiptoe, she lifted her mouth to his in a long, fierce kiss. He didn't move a muscle and she knew he meant to humiliate her completely.

'Proof,' she said grimly, her fingers marvelling at the smoothness of his jaw.

'Yes?' he enquired lazily.

'You devil!' she glared. He laughed huskily and she quivered when he jerked her tighter to him roughly, the lines of his body intimate and menacing. Through her sped the heat of need and for once she gave in to it. 'Proof,' she whispered. Her hands slid into his hair, moulding into the curve of his head, stroking the nape of his neck. And she pulled his head down to kiss his hot lips then boldly slid her tongue between his teeth.

He pushed her away.

'Oh, God!' she moaned. 'You're not going to reject me!'

'It means so much to you?' he asked softly.

'Are you trying to break me?' she answered, miserable that he should be so brutal and ruthless with her life.

'I'm doing what I always do,' he said cynically. 'Getting the best of the deal. If I marry you, it'll be forever. I will not put Melanie through any more divorced-parent scenarios. Understand? Whatever happens, we stick together and put up a show.'

'Understood,' Rosalind said nervously, shutting her mind to the long years ahead.

'We will make a contract, legal and binding,' he said. 'You'll get half my wealth, a recognised place in society and no more worries for the rest of your life. You needn't even work, though I have no objections if you want to, providing Melanie is brought up well and cared for—and I believe you'll do that. You fuss over her like a mother already.'

She held down the urge to groan. 'Yes,' she said dully.

'Well, I suppose I have no alternative,' he said casually. Rosalind scowled at him but his steady glance didn't waver. 'We'll announce our engagement and have a party this week and you can display to everyone there how much you love me.'

'This week!' She found she couldn't break away from his mesmeric, brooding stare. 'Yes,' she whispered.

'You must do your best. We have to persuade Blanche that her services are no longer needed.'

Rosalind gave a choked gasp. 'You bastard!' she breathed.

'That's me,' he agreed. 'But you must agree that she's got to go.'

'Don't you pension her off?' Rosalind asked sullenly. 'Is this all your discarded mistresses get—a public humiliation and the cold shoulder?'

'You want me to pay her?' he snarled. 'Listen, Rosalind. Don't you feel pity for that steel magnolia. She's as sly as a swamp snake and twice as slippery.'

Her fists uncurled on his warm chest and she pushed the flat of her palms against the living wall of muscle, his arms tightening around her so that she arched her supple body back. 'Let me go.' She wriggled to no avail.

'Not yet. You need to know Blanche's role in my life.'

'I should have thought that was obvious,' she said painfully.

'No. She merely provided evidence for my divorce. Annie wanted to keep me tied to her so that I'd never remarry. I think she was afraid I'd have other children and my fortune would have to be shared around.'

No, thought Rosalind. It was because she feared the truth of Melanie's birth would come out and Chance would cease to provide for them both. 'Didn't you want to be free?' she asked.

'It didn't matter a damn to me, one way or the other. But when it became clear I'd never have a normal relationship with my daughter I decided it would be better if we made a clean break. As a southern gentleman, I had to be the guilty party, so I had to force her hand. I arranged to be caught with Blanche.'

'Arranged?' frowned Rosalind.

'She was willing to be "the other woman", hoping it would become true,' he said drily. 'I asked Blanche because there were no other women in my life to ask. Do you hear that?'

'You're surely not suggesting that you didn't play around during your marriage,' she said coldly.

'It's possible, Rosalind,' he growled. 'That's why I'm so very hungry now.'

'Oh. You've been totally celibate since your divorce? What about your friendly neighbour? You go over next door and sit in her kitchen and chat with her over the *café au lait* and *beignets*, do you?' she asked scathingly.

He laughed, and licked her sulky mouth. Her shuddering response invited his tongue to explore further.
'Blanche and I talk about take-over bids. I'm trying to
buy her out,' he whispered against her lips, his breath
hot and urgent. He slid his hands to her buttocks and
massaged her rounded cheeks, lazily smiling with satisfaction at her increased rate of breathing. 'Look. I
don't want her next door because of her unwelcome influence on Melanie. I think this marriage of ours will
force her to accept my price. I've been trying to get rid
of her for years and have had to keep her sweet. I'm
sure she'll go when you move in permanently. The
woman has her pride.'

He shifted his weight, the hard ridge of his hip grazing
against hers, and then his thigh was between hers and
she could feel the hardness of him, pressing against her.
The blood pounded in her ears at the persistent rhythm
of his hands over her buttocks, pushing her hard into
his body. She leaned back, and his mouth swooped to
the low neckline of her dress, delving into her hot, moist
breasts.

'Chance!' she gasped softly.

One hand slid up her body, shaping into its curves
with a controlled violence that terrified and excited her.
Then she felt his fingers tug at her chin, opening her
mouth to his ravaging tongue, the insolent, suggestive
kiss.

She was moist, receptive, wanting and waiting. She
hardly knew that they had moved from the path, only
dimly aware of the rasp of the cool grass against her
naked back and that Chance was half lying on her, his
fingers roughly jerking down the straps of her dress.

His mouth was on her breasts, suckling and tugging
and awakening them till she felt within her a sensation
of being so sensual and filled with eroticism that it made
her want to be everything he needed—mistress, wanton

lover, abandoned siren. She hungered for him and saw no reason to hold back.

Her fingers undid the buttons of his shirt, slowly, while the torment of her body continued. Her lids became heavy and half closed, so she was forced to frown in concentration and take even greater care over each reluctant button. She slid the tips of her fingers inside his shirt and contacted the gorgeous satin skin, then the small, tight crests of his nipples. He flinched and she looked up and smiled with a woman's pleasure at the miracle of a powerful and virile man's dependence on the touch of a female.

Gently she unravelled his tie and threw it carelessly away. Her mouth touched his throat.

'That's enough,' he said hoarsely. 'Proof enough. I accept your proposal.'

She felt his body leave her, the longed-for pressure lifted from her thighs. Slowly and with difficulty she forced her eyes to open, feeling drugged by his wandering hands and the male smell of him. 'What—what—what do you mean, enough?' she said in a slurred voice.

She could see his shoulders rising and falling. She knew he wanted her. So why, oh, why, she moaned in secret frustration, didn't he make love to her?

'Enough is enough.' He held out his hand. Languidly she took it and then, angry, pulled—hoping he'd return to her. He stumbled a little and recovered himself then jerked her to her feet where she stood swaying and confused. Chance laughed softly, kissing her in a long, slow forever kiss. 'You've certainly learnt a lot since we last met,' he said huskily. 'I think I'm going to get my money's worth.'

'You swine!' Her hand flew up and he parried it, gripping her wrist so tightly that she winced and felt her knees buckle.

'Let's get this relationship straight, shall we?' he murmured. 'I'm the one who calls the shots. You take your clothes off—or let me do so—whenever I want, and you get all the goodies in exchange. You can think I'm a bastard and you can say so in private, but never in public and you never hit me. Got that?'

'You're hurting me!' she gasped.

'Of course. I'm not a real gentleman, am I?' he snapped, letting her go instantly and meeting her angry eyes with a challenging look.

'That doesn't give you the right to treat me roughly during our marriage,' she said shakily. 'Do that and I leave you.'

'Leave me and I'll drag you back by your hair,' he snarled.

She felt only despair, flowing in over the aching void that he'd opened up within her. 'How can I hate you and want you?' she moaned.

'I ask myself the same question,' he said tightly. 'I doubt we'll ever answer it.'

'My God! You look sensational!' Chance rose from the eighteenth-century walnut chair, staring at Rosalind as she descended the short flight of stairs which led to the down-river sitting-room.

And so do you, she thought to herself. He wore a new tuxedo which shaped to his body like no other and she wanted desperately to run towards him and run her hands over the tantalising swell of his chest. He had planted his feet slightly apart, his head held high, the bronzed curve of his throat infinitely touchable above the wickedly bright red floppy bow that only Chance could have worn and got away with.

Her hungry eyes feasted on the arrogant, cruel curl of his mouth, the straight nose and dark, hot eyes beneath the intensely black brows. And instead of running forwards to push back the lock of night-black hair that had fallen on to his forehead she smiled coolly.

'You like it?'

'I suppose I ought to because it probably cost me a fortune,' he said drily. 'But then, it wouldn't look half as good on any other woman. Come here.'

Obediently, she steeled herself and walked towards him. Since he had accepted her proposal beneath Oak Alley, he had been absent from the house and she and Melanie had mooned around like lost sheep. But then he'd phoned saying the party had been arranged and their engagement had been announced. Melanie was thrilled and that took away Rosalind's resentment that Chance had not consulted her at all—and that she had been left to deal with the dozens of phone calls that his announcement had provoked.

Of Blanche she had heard nothing.

'Verrry nice. Turn around.' He fastened the emerald necklace around her throat and she wondered if he remembered where he had kissed her when it lay on her body before. Apparently he did. His fingers stroked the upswelling of her breasts and the breathing on the back of her neck became hotter and more erratic.

'I told the saleswoman I wanted something red, cut low and tight,' she said scathingly. 'I thought it would please your taste.'

'A whore's dress for a whore,' he murmured.

She swung around, her mouth open in astonishment. 'What did you call me?' she demanded.

'Don't forget I'm buying you,' he said, his hand insolently cupping around her breast. 'This, and...' to her bottom '...this and...' to her thighs '...oh, Rosalind,' he murmured. 'Your eyes dilated so fast I thought someone had turned the light out.'

'You are a bastard!' she whispered, seething with anger.

He chuckled and slid his hand down to her silk-clad leg, lifting the material of her dress so that it slipped sensually upwards, accompanied by his delicate and audacious touch.

'Mmm. Sexy. Yes, I'm a bastard with money and you're marrying me for it. Got your public role clear? You adore me and you can't keep your hands off me.'

'Can't we just settle for simpering wonder?' she asked sourly, pulling her skirt straight.

'Blanche wouldn't believe it,' he said laconically.

She groaned. 'Not Blanche!'

'Of course. Let's get it over with.'

'Where are we going?' she asked sullenly.

'Soften that grumpy mouth of yours.' He frowned when she continued to pout and pushed her against the wall, pressing his body hard into hers as he worked his magic on her mouth and reduced her to a quivering mass of female hormones.

'Melanie...' she croaked, when he came up for air.

'She's in the car, waiting.' His finger tipped up her chin and he nodded. 'Yes. Softer. But not quite right...'

He hauled her to him, just holding her, just kissing, nothing more. But it was the way he did it, sweet and gentle, tender and caressing, that released all her tension and made her dreamily respond as if he'd spent hours arousing her. She loved him, she thought raggedly. So very, very much.

Unsteadily, she let him cuddle her when they walked to the car. He stumbled as if he'd been drinking, but she knew his breath had tasted sweet and fresh and she was bewildered at his dazed expression until she realised he was putting on a show for anyone who happened to be watching.

The thought hurt her more than she imagined it could. She knew that was because she wanted him to be *really* knocked out by her. It almost made her determined to capture him in some way, to make him need her. She winced. She was getting devious.

'Oh, Rosalind! You're so beautiful!' breathed the impatiently waiting Melanie ecstatically.

'You look like a million dollars, Miss Ros'lin',' smiled Kate. 'And so much in love. We sure are happy for y'all.'

'Thank you, Melanie. Thank you, Kate,' smiled Rosalind warmly. 'I'm very happy to be staying.'

'Where we going, where we going?' cried Melanie, jumping up and down.

'Surprise, sweetheart,' grinned Chance. 'Rosalind, we'll sit in the back with Melanie. She'll keep us in order. Kate, take the front with Johnny.'

'I'd like to offer my congratulations, Mr Chance,' said Johnny warmly. 'You couldn't have done better in a million years.' He turned to Rosalind. 'Miss Rosalind, you've got yourself a fine man. A fine man.'

'Thank you,' said Rosalind, charmed by the chauffeur's enthusiasm. Someone thought highly of Chance, at least.

Nervous and excited, she sank into the deep, soft grey kid seat. Chance opened the champagne as they moved off.

'A toast to my two darling girls,' he said, with a piratical grin. 'The two women I will love to the end of my life.'

Rosalind's face almost lost its smile. She wondered whom he was talking about since it certainly wasn't her. Melanie squealed with delight that she was allowed some champagne and sipped it as if it were liquid gold, her eyes huge as they stared solemnly at her father over the glass.

'It is for always, isn't it, Daddy?' she asked breathlessly.

'Always,' he promised. 'Isn't it, Rosalind?'

Oh, dear heaven, she thought. What a prison sentence. 'I will never leave you,' she said in a husky voice, touching Melanie's soft, downy cheek lightly.

'I'm so happy,' Melanie sighed. 'I feel like dancing on the roof of the car.'

'Save your feet and the paintwork,' laughed Chance. 'There'll be dancing enough soon.'

'Have you hired a room in a hotel?' Melanie asked. Chance shook his head. 'I know! In a mansion in St Charles?'

'No. It's...somewhere I own.'

'Oh. In your offices,' said Melanie, sounding a little disappointed.

Rosalind looked out of the car window, feeling puzzled. They weren't going in the direction of New Orleans at all. And the road they were taking seemed to be leading to the river and the old cotton wharves.

'Ohh!' she cried, her eyes widening. 'Look, Melanie, look!'

'A steamboat! A steamboat! We're partying on a *paddlewheeler*! Oh, Daddy, it's the most exciting thing in the world, you and Ros getting married and me dancin' an' list'nin' to jazz, an'—oh, look at them there pretty balloons an' the streamers, Ros! Oh, oh, oh!'

Both Rosalind and Chance were laughing in delight at Melanie's total happiness and her excited delivery, and then their glances met and for a moment Rosalind thought she saw a hurt, agonised yearning dimming Chance's sparking eyes, but he was hugging Melanie, his head buried in her neck, and his expression was impossible to see.

'Come on, come on!' yelled Melanie, racing to the gangplank the moment the car had rolled to a stop.

'I'll go, Mr Chance,' laughed Kate, picking up her skirts and running after Melanie. 'You do it more dignified, like,' she yelled back.

Chance held out his hand to Rosalind and she slipped her legs out of the car. When she stood up, she was in his embrace, and she automatically jerked away, but his hand ruthlessly pushed her into him again.

'You love me. Damn you, remember! In public, you love me,' he said savagely.

Under the eyes of their guests on the steamboat, she suffered his kiss in silence, hurting with the pain that drove the double-edged sword into her. Double-edged because she wanted him to kiss her and yet hated the farce of doing so.

'It's all right,' she said, when he finally let her go. 'No one will ever know my real feelings for you. I promise you that.'

It was true, of course, she thought, as they strolled to the boat, arms lovingly around one another, giving each other fond glances every few paces. No one would ever realise that she loved him with all her heart and had done so since she was eighteen years old. She could look at him and mean what her eyes said. How he managed to appear so convincing she couldn't imagine.

However, the atmosphere of the party made it all so much easier. People were laughing and happy for them both, his friends genuinely delighted—and delightful. Rosalind relaxed, beginning to feel that she could bear it all, and that maybe she could make some good friends of the people he knew and thus ease her emptiness of spirit.

The steamboat gave a deep blast of its horn that made everyone shriek and then it began to move in stately fashion up-river. Rosalind was whirled into a group of Cajun dancers who tried to teach her the complicated arm-wrestling style of dancing and then she was extracted by a laughing Chance who proceeded to kiss her till she felt dizzy and the applause of the surrounding guests made her pink with embarrassment.

'You're doing fine,' he said huskily.

She looked deep into his eyes. He appeared to be a man in love, the dark velvet of his eyes making her tremble. 'Oh, Chance,' she whispered, her fingertips tentatively touching his mouth.

Streamers cascaded down on them. They stood swaying to the music, oblivious of everyone and everything. Around them, balloons popped as loudly as the champagne, people milled around the brightly lit boat, watching the jugglers and acrobats and the magic show. The world-famous male tenor began to sing Italian love-songs and Rosalind lifted her arms around Chance's neck, holding him tightly, and they still stared in each other's eyes tenderly, adoringly.

For the duration of this wonderful evening, she thought drowsily, she could pretend.

'Come outside and see the sunset on the river,' he whispered in her ear.

And they stumbled out, to the distant sound of much indulgent laughter. He led her to the rail and they watched the white water tumbling over the paddlewheel as it churned through the still, silent Mississippi and the acres of sugarcane. The river curved sinuously ahead in a dazzling, glassy sheet that was slowly turning a deep rose-pink. An occasional mullet disturbed the smooth surface, leaping a couple of feet in the air to plop con-tentedly back again. Other than that, all was calm.

'It's wonderful,' she breathed. 'Utterly perfect.'

'And so are you,' said Chance, maintaining the pretence.

His hand rested lightly on her spine, spreading warm and familiar, and at that moment she wanted time to stop and not to go on because ahead she could see only heartache while on this magical river in the sunset she could believe that he really did love her and she and her child were both cared for, equally.

'What . . . oh, Chance!' she laughed gently, seeing that he had drawn up some of the wide pink ribbons decor-ating the boat and had tied her to the rail.

He smiled, neatly tying a bow around her waist. And knelt, presenting her with a box. 'For you, Rosalind.'

Trembling, she took it. When she opened it and saw the enormous diamond and emerald ring, she wanted to weep. 'It's lovely,' she breathed in awe. Her eyes filled treacherously.

'You will be my wife. You should wear it,' said Chance quietly, looking up at her, his eyes haunting her with their dark desire. 'It was my mother's. She adored it. She told me once that emeralds are for love. And diamonds are forever.'

'No, no,' she moaned.

'Yes,' he said grimly, standing up and taking the ring out of the box. He caught her limp hand and pushed the ring on to the third finger with a vehement action. 'The irony isn't lost on me.'

The tears trickled down her face as emotion claimed her. She felt him untying the ribbons and leading her along the deck then, stopping to kiss her when others blundered past. There was silence again and he lifted her in his arms, carrying her to a cabin door and kicking it open.

A heavy perfume came to her nostrils and she blinked away her tears to see better. It looked as if there were hundreds of roses in the cabin.

She felt stunned. 'All these roses,' she gasped.

'This is your cabin,' he said curtly. 'It's for you to use, to freshen up, to hide in. I thought you might need somewhere.' Gently he laid her on the day-bed, its silk-lined embroidered drapes pinned with dozens of full-blown roses.

'That—that was thoughtful,' she quavered.

He grimaced. 'If there's anything you need . . .'

'To make the party memorable?' she asked softly.

There was a long, long silence. 'Yes,' he said in a deep, shaking voice. 'Whatever you want I will give you if it is in my power.'

'I want you,' someone whispered through her own lips, the voice coming from somewhere deep within the core of her body.

CHAPTER SEVEN

CHANCE looked down on the flushed Rosalind, his eyes guarded. 'That's a little inconvenient,' he said hoarsely. 'Blanche and I——'

Spitting with rage, Rosalind tried to sit up, only to find Chance's restraining hand on her chest pushing her back again. 'Blanche and you!' she grated in fury. 'This is *my* engagement party and I'm trying to pretend I love you and you're not making it any easier with this Blanche and you business!'

Unaccountably, he laughed, low and husky, a sound that reached into her intensely sensitive mind and made her madder still. But he reached out and took her hand, bringing it to his groin where, for a brief second, she felt the scorching heat of male virility beneath the black linen cloth, leaping with hard, unnerving power into her palm.

'That is to tell you that I want you,' he said in a gravel-laden growl. 'And I could have you now if I chose. But I want you to know that I can control myself as much as any man—more than any man, if necessary——'

'Because Blanche is ready and waiting in an identical cabin?' she asked, miserably recognising how stupid she sounded, but wrung with jealousy, and incapable of holding back the words.

'You're insulting me with your idiocy,' he said curtly. 'She and I are going to have a little chat and then you're going to knock her flat with your personal rendition of the loving, wanton whore whom I'm more than eager to marry. Play the part well, Rosalind. There's more to come.'

She lay there for a while after he had left, feeling ashamed of her silly accusation and getting her blood-pressure back to near normal. And then she went on deck again to laugh and dance and to seek refuge by watching Melanie give an impromptu performance of her own—a dance with her adoring father.

'Nauseating little brat, isn't she?' came Blanche's honey-sweet voice.

Rosalind almost gave herself away by the fiery blaze that leapt into her eyes. 'I think she's a cracker,' replied Rosalind haughtily, all her motherly feelings deeply insulted.

'Ah, Blanche,' murmured Chance. 'Is this just girl-talk or can I claim this...?' He looked at Rosalind and the tip of his tongue slipped out to touch his top lip speculatively. 'This beautiful possession of mine,' he murmured.

Rosalind's eyes blazed at his patronising air and the claim of ownership. 'You're going to have to do better than that to possess me,' she complained, trying to remember the role. 'My lover needs to be tender and passionate and eager to please me.'

He laughed unpleasantly and there was suddenly an air of crackling energy about him as he looked at her, the sexual tension stringing Rosalind's nerves into thin, brittle wires that vibrated with every flicker of his eyelashes.

'Hell,' he whispered, his gaze glued to her startled blue eyes. 'That sounds exciting. Come here and I'll do just that. How,' he wondered, as if in a daze, 'could I ever have known any other women existed?'

'Chance,' pouted Blanche.

To Rosalind's untold private joy, he pushed Blanche impatiently to one side and stood within a foot of Rosalind, the raw greed that consumed them both elec-trifying and thickening the air between them. His lashes fluttered as if he was slipping into a beautiful dream and she clutched her breast to contain her heartache.

He looked around and seemed to come to the realisation that they were surrounded by groups of people discreetly trying not to notice what was going on. He scowled and grinned his crooked, pirate's grin that made Rosalind's knees buckle.

'Steady, sweetheart. Throw some cold water on me or something,' he groaned.

The pain left her eyes. 'Allow me,' she said grimly, reaching for a glass of champagne.

As quick as lightning, he caught her hand and smiled sweetly at her. 'Thank you, darling. Careful!' he laughed, when the liquid slopped. 'Shaky hand?' He grinned wickedly. 'Me too. To us,' he said silkily, forcing her to stretch her arm so that he could sip the drink. 'Our eternal happiness... Now you.'

Foiled, loathing the charade, she finished the champagne, her furious eyes promising him revenge. Chance lifted an eyebrow at her. There was a slight pressure on her hand which felt as if he might break her knuckles and reluctantly she decided to obey him, if only to get rid of Blanche once and for all.

She blinked. It was like a lightning bolt hitting her dull brain. That was actually what she wanted—no more Blanche, no more southern sirens. Just her and Melanie and Chance. They'd work something out somehow.

'I had the impression you disliked Chance,' the woman said sulkily.

'Did I fool you too?' said Rosalind, managing a smile. She decided to make a real effort. 'Why,' she said to the astonished woman, 'don't you know a man just loves running after women? Chance is crazy about me because he's never sure where he stands. Isn't that right, darling?' she murmured provocatively, tapping his mouth saucily with her forefinger.

His teeth gently savaged it and her eyes flickered with desire at the throbbing of her pulses. 'Melanie's fallen asleep,' he said hoarsely. 'Let's go home and walk naked down to the river.'

'Chance!' protested Blanche, shocked.

'The mosquitoes would have a field day,' grinned Rosalind.

'So we run,' he suggested, his eyes telling her that he didn't care, one way or another.

'Really——' began Blanche.

'You stand there much longer, Blanche,' he breathed, his dark gaze hotly riveted to Rosalind's, 'and you'll hear far more intimate plans than those.' His hand curled around Rosalind's neck and she imperceptibly tipped her head back.

'You can have my house at the price you want,' muttered Blanche. 'Why you never took what I offered, I don't know!'

'Are you talking only about the extortionate value you set on your plantation?' he drawled.

'It doesn't matter,' snapped Blanche. 'I would have liked to know if you were as good as the rumours say you are.'

'Goodbye,' Chance said meaningfully.

The woman walked to the far end of the boat, her head held high, and Rosalind felt sorry for her. But she'd latched on to something that puzzled her. 'Didn't you ever make love to Blanche?' she asked slowly, as she and Chance swayed to the rhythm of the music.

'Is there a law that says I must?'

'You need women and she was available,' she argued. 'You're not the kind of man to turn that sort of offer down.'

'If that's what you want to believe, then I can't stop you,' he said with a shrug.

'I don't *want* to believe it,' she said in irritation. 'I'd had the impression——'

'Without evidence?' he asked in a hard and dangerous tone. 'That's how people get accused of things they didn't do. That's how they get shut away for years with the whole of society smug and satisfied that a criminal is no longer at large.'

'Are you saying you're innocent on both charges?' she asked in astonishment.

He scowled. 'Who, me?' he mocked. 'Careful. People are staring. Back to work. Pretend you love me. Dance with me properly,' he said huskily, beginning to sway sensually against her. 'Drive me wild.'

Rosalind gritted her teeth and forced herself to do so. Chance's big hands clamped around her back and thrust hard so that she could feel how tense his muscles were. And she wondered how he could move with the hard swell of need pressing against her pelvis.

'You're doing a good job,' he husked.

She grabbed his head and put her mouth to his ear. 'I want Blanche to get out of our lives,' she muttered. 'Not to leave the field clear for me, you understand, but to stop gossip.'

He bent his head till their foreheads touched and stared into her eyes, mesmerising her, so that the party, the chatter and the music flowed around them like the river and yet she was oblivious of it all.

The lights were dimmed. Above sparkled tiny stars. Rosalind felt a tug of heartbreaking romance shafting through her body. She loved Chance. Could she hold the dream in her head and fool herself that he loved her too?

'Pretend to me,' she said shakily. 'Pretend you love me.'

'I am,' he muttered into her hair.

'No, I mean . . . I mean *really* pretend.'

'So that you can live with your conscience for marrying a man for his money?' he asked tightly.

'Does it matter why?' she whispered, her fingers stroking his proud cheekbones. 'Can't we wrap ourselves in a world of pretence?'

'I tried before,' he muttered, staring over her head coldly. 'It didn't work.' He drew in his breath when her mouth accidentally touched his throat. 'Perhaps the sex will be better,' he said harshly.

She winced. 'Please don't be so brutal.'

'You're the one who made the business proposition. If I'm to keep my sanity, I have to remember that,' he said grimly.

They clung together as if nothing would ever prise them apart. But their bodies were cold and unresponsive and there was no magic left in the starry night.

'I want to go to the cabin. You said I could use it as a retreat,' she said sullenly, when her body began to ache from tension.

'You'll stay in my arms,' he said ruthlessly in her ear, turning it into a travesty of a kiss for the benefit of his friends. 'You'll act as if you want me. Little loving touches, long loving looks. Let your hands wander a bit more. Kiss me sometimes. This is beginning to look like a dance between——'

'Cleopatra and the asp,' she muttered.

He kissed her hard, his hand gently fondling her bottom. 'Do as you're darn well told,' he growled.

She kissed his cheek and slid her mouth to his ear, which she nibbled for a while. The farce continued. She loved him and she hated him in equal measures and the poignant situation was bringing her close to despair.

At last the soft rush of water over the paddle changed to a roar and Rosalind realising that the paddleboat was mooring by the jetty they'd started from. Couples took their leave, broke them apart and kissed them both and left. They were the last on the dance-floor, still dreamily swaying to the sleazy sensuality of the saxophone.

Rosalind felt a dreadful sadness wash over her. The party was over. It was time to wake up to the masquerade.

'Chance. Stop this now,' she said sharply.

'I'm enjoying it.'

'You don't sound as if you are. And Melanie ought to be taken back to her bed.'

'I wasn't impressed with your final performance,' he scowled.

'I'm not used to pretending emotions I don't feel,' she muttered.

He abandoned her, going to the band and thanking them, slipping them all an extra bonus. He woke Kate and Melanie and jerked his head insolently at Rosalind. She sullenly followed him thinking that from now on life would go downhill rapidly.

He tucked Melanie over his shoulder and she trustingly fell asleep again, murmuring how happy she was when he pushed her into the car. Exhausted from holding herself rigid for so long, Rosalind promptly fell asleep too, the moment her head hit the soft upholstery.

She woke at one stage and felt Chance's arms around her, lifting her, and she kept her eyes shut while he strode over the gravel, up the wooden steps and across the gallery to her bedroom where he put her down gently on the bed.

Her whole skin surface tingled because she knew he hadn't left—she could sense his body still sitting beside her. Then his lips brushed her forehead, her nose and her mouth and came back for more, his lips soft and hungry, his tongue sliding inside so sweetly that she clutched him and bolted open her eyes.

'Go back to sleep, Rosalind,' he growled. 'I prefer you that way.'

'Out of my room!' she croaked nervously.

'It's mine. As you are,' he said coldly. 'Don't ever forget that.'

To prove his words, he let his hands drift over her body, touching every single inch until she was clenching her fists so that she wouldn't beg him to stay. She'd learnt her lesson from the last time. He just liked the power that her submission gave him. So in an agonised silence she suffered his touch and then he stood up and left.

In the early morning, he came in and found her sitting in the rocking-chair by the window, still wearing her dress from the night before. She hadn't slept and that was obvious, her accusing, darkened eyes glancing scathingly at him then shifting away.

'I'll be out today,' he said quietly. 'I'll be back this afternoon.' He waited again. 'Get yourself changed and showered, Rosalind. Pay some attention to my child, even if you can't bring yourself to be civil to me.'

'Whores don't need to be civil to their clients,' she snapped.

He blanched. 'You haven't begun to whore for me yet,' he muttered. He considered her for several seconds and then turned on his heel. 'You'll know all about it when you do.'

She stayed where she was until he had driven away and then forced herself to be bright and cheerful for her blissfully happy daughter. But Rosalind felt extraordinarily tired, and after a morning talking about the party and riding around the plantation she pleaded a headache and went to lie on her bed while Melanie read contentedly in the shade of an old magnolia tree and waited for her father to return.

Late afternoon, she heard the sound of a car and ran to the window, watching Melanie run into his arms and squeal in delight when he whirled her in the air. She observed them closely. Melanie was telling him about her day and he was gently stroking her hair, a smile of fatherly adoration on his beaming face. His eyes followed her every moment. Any observer would say that he was crazy about his daughter.

She watched them running to the river hand in hand and her eyes grew wistful. If only they could be a real family. Mother, father, daughter. Rosalind turned her face to the curtain and sobbed into its folds. There was no hope of that.

Hot and sticky, she went to lie in the marble bathtub, deliberately blanking her mind to anything other than the lap of the cool water against her body.

Chilled, she suddenly realised she'd been in there ages, and that the house was silent. She dressed, wondering where Chance and Melanie were because there was no sign of them in the house. The sun began to sink and she worried that it was almost dark and they had no torches with them. Night fell fast, this far south.

And she spent the next hour trying not to panic. Chance was with Melanie. There was no danger. Chance was with her. They'd gone for a walk and were having precious time together.

Or... he could have been careless again. They could be injured, lost... worse. Rosalind went pale. She paced up and down the gallery wondering how long she should wait before she called the plantation manager. And her patience would hold no longer. There was something wrong. The two people she loved dearly were in trouble and she couldn't bear it. Frantic now, she turned, intending to make the phone call for help and at that moment she heard voices murmuring somewhere in the darkness of the garden.

'Melanie! Chance! Oh, darlings——!' She stopped in her headlong flight down the stairs, confronted by a surprised Chance—and Blanche. 'Oh! I thought *you'd* left!' she said rudely.

'I'm going in an hour,' said a subdued Blanche.

'Where's Melanie?' she fired at Chance, agitated.

'I sent her home ages ago. Isn't she here?' he frowned.

Her mouth dried. 'No,' she whispered, her blue eyes angry and upset. 'What have you done with her?'

'Thrown her in a bayou,' he growled. 'What the hell do you think?'

Blanche stiffened. 'That child is so self-centred, she can't *bear* it when her daddy speaks to anyone else. She said she was going to walk slow till we finished what we were doing.'

'My God, Chance Decatur!' seethed Rosalind, grabbing a torch from the hook on the wall, all her control slipping in her anxiety. 'You leave a seven-year-old child out in the dark so you can act out one of your famous goodbye scenes and play *stud*?'

'Rosalind!' roared Chance, striding after her and whirling her around. 'You'll apologise to Blanche.'

'Yes. Yes. I'm sorry!' Ashamed of her crude words, Rosalind lowered her anguished eyes. 'I've been worried sick——'

'Stay here!' he ordered.

'No! I want to come,' she snapped, wrenching her arm away. Chance cursed and stormed into the house and she gave a sob, then ran towards the trees, calling Melanie's name. Hearing the sound of running feet, she turned to see Chance racing towards her, a shot-gun slung over his shoulder.

'Go back to the house.' Chance caught her roughly and pushed her in that direction, but she stumbled and his arm snaked out to save her from falling. 'Please,' he muttered. 'I think she's taken the boat. I thought I heard the outboard motor. Melanie was angry when Blanche came across me by accident.'

'Accident?' she cried hysterically. 'Do you imagine she ever did anything by accident? And what do you mean, angry?'

'I invited Blanche back for a farewell drink. Melanie got protective of you,' he growled. 'Blanche hadn't wanted to meet me again after last night. She was having a last look at the river before she left for Dallas. I suggested she come back with me to the house to make her peace with us all and that's when Melanie ran off ahead. Now stay. This could take some time.'

'She might be anywhere in the creeks. Anywhere,' Rosalind said miserably. The bayous were almost impossible to distinguish one from the other. People could get lost out there, really lost. 'She's out there in the darkness all alone!' she cried. And there were the alligators... She let out a distraught moan. 'Take me with you!' she demanded, clinging relentlessly to his arm.

Without gentleness, he peeled off each finger and pushed her away. 'You'd get in the way,' he snapped. 'Check the house. Check the outbuildings. Ask around. She could be hiding to alarm me.'

'She wouldn't do that——'

'Oh, yes, she would. She'd even throw herself out of a tree to keep you,' he said grimly. 'She's capable of anything.'

Rosalind froze. 'What did you say?' she gasped.

He frowned impatiently. 'You heard,' he muttered.

'Tell me,' she demanded. 'I've got to know. Now.'

'Quickly, then. She was beside herself when I sat in that tree with her and told her you were leaving. She's clever; I suppose she worked it out that you'd hover by her bedside or whatever if she was injured. She told me later that it never occurred to her she might have been killed. She'd do anything to keep you at Sans Souci. Almost,' he said, his brow furrowed, 'as much as you're prepared to sacrifice for her sake. There's a bond between you two as strong as life itself.'

Rosalind winced. 'Find her,' she whispered. 'For heaven's sake, find her.'

He nodded. 'If you don't hear a single shot in fifteen minutes, get hold of the men and organise a search party. Got that?' He gave her a rough shake because she seemed numb with terror.

'Yes!' she said, trying to pull herself together.

'Ros.'

'What? What?' she cried in agitation.

'She'll be OK. I'll find her. And when I do,' he said, changing his gentle tone to a grim one, 'I'll flay her alive!'

'No, don't hurt her, don't hurt my Melly!' whispered Rosalind.

His eyes glittered. 'Figure of speech,' he snarled. 'You still don't trust me to protect my own daughter. To *hell* with you.'

She watched him go and then automatically carried out the search, knowing she wouldn't find her little girl. Then she waited on the gallery as the sweltering night grew darker and the stars filled the sky with pin-pricks of light and the moths fluttered against the window-panes behind her, desperate to reach the bright light beyond.

It was like her, she thought. She was attracted to something that would ultimately destroy her and perhaps Melanie too. If he'd been a normal, loving father, she would never have needed to stay and Melanie wouldn't have been so defiant about running into the bayou because she felt insecure about her father's relationships with women.

Suddenly, she strained against the balustrade. Lights were dancing in the darkness. She flew down the steps three at a time in their direction, gasping from the transition from fan-cooled air to the oppressive torrid threat of a night-time storm.

'Melanie! Melanie!' she yelled, pleading with the Fates all the time that she was safe.

She came to a grinding halt. Chance was carrying her daughter's limp, lifeless body in his arms. Rosalind gave a little moan, reached out a fluttering, feeble hand and fell to the ground in a dead faint.

'Ros. Ros, for God's sake, open your eyes!'

They snapped open and she sat bolt upright to find herself on her own bed. 'Melanie——!' A firm hand—Chance's—pushed her back.

'She's fine. I told you she would be,' said Chance curtly. 'She was frightened and whimpering like a little kitten and I told her stories and we made our way back and she's going to be eternally sorry she worried us so much.'

Rosalind caught his arms and half pushed herself up. 'What do you mean, she's going to be sorry?' she whispered, appalled.

'I mean,' he said tightly, 'that she'll never forgive herself for worrying you so badly.'

'I was half out of my mind,' she cried hoarsely. 'Where is she? I want to——'

'No. She's asleep, absolutely exhausted from fear and crying. I promised I'd talk to you on her behalf. You're to leave her alone.'

'Why?' she asked shakily.

'Rosalind,' he frowned irritably, 'I've just explained——'

'No. What reason could you have for not letting me see my own—goddaughter?' she said, stumbling for a moment. Her eyes registered alarm. His eyes looked daggers at her. 'I want to see her!' she demanded.

'No,' he said stubbornly, holding her on the pillows. 'I refuse to allow you to wake her. I am her father. Mine is the final word in this house.'

'But—but Melanie is in my care too.' Rosalind pushed back her tumbled hair, her face sulky. To her alarm, she saw the desire spill into his eyes, felt the slide of his hands on her shoulders and gulped. 'I—I won't wake her.'

He smiled lazily. 'No. Because you won't be going to look at her. She is perfectly all right and she is asleep and you will wait until the morning to see her. You will be too busy to worry about her. We have some unfinished business. *Business*, you understand. You and I are going to make a journey of our own.'

She stared at him with loathing. 'At a time like this? You must be mad!' she croaked.

'Melanie is sleeping. She is safe. Mad, I might be, but I'll have you tonight and take the edge off my hunger so I can get the world back into perspective again,' he said savagely.

His hand slowly moved down the length of her face and Rosalind tensed with terror and anticipation. His black hair tumbled on to his forehead and she reached up to push it away with a gentle gesture then hastily retracted her hand. Without hurrying, he let his fingers skim her throat, but instead of being a loving gesture it seemed sinister.

'You showed a depth of loving towards my child that I want to possess,' he ground out. 'I'm jealous. I want it, Rosalind. Me. I'm going to eat you alive, inch by inch.'

She tried to look away from his hard, glittering eyes and couldn't. She attempted to speak, but only a moan broke from her parched lips. 'Chaaance,' she croaked as he licked her lips for her, moistening them with a sweetness she wanted to know forever. 'Please don't do this,' she said unhappily. 'Any other time, but not now.'

'I must,' he muttered, and when she shuddered at the exhalation of his words on her acutely sensitized throat he gave a low growl in his throat, his face almost brutal in its intense concentration.

'I'm not ready for——'

'I am. One of us is sufficient,' he said callously.

His hand coaxed away the fine Egyptian cotton sheet which covered her form. Rosalind whimpered. He seemed neither to care nor notice if she was aroused. And yet when he tried to undo the buttons on her dress he was gentle, using the lightest of touches and an infuriatingly slow movement to do so.

'You think that if you seduce me then I will be crazy for you, don't you?' she said jerkily, her breath uneven from sheer terror.

'Yes.' Insolently, he smiled and ripped open her dress. 'That's the general idea.'

She lay there miserably while he slowly, inevitably, aroused her body, not doing anything to encourage him. Separate from her mind, she felt herself moving reluctantly into his arms and the delicate, tantalisingly gentle kisses branding her skin. But she held back. Too much had happened to sour this moment.

'Give in, damn you,' he muttered.

'I can't,' she whispered. 'I won't.'

'You think I'm a womaniser. You're mistaken.'

'The girls in the office? The women we kept at bay? Were they all fictions of my imagination?' she asked resentfully.

'No,' he said gently. 'I had a grand time till my eyes settled on you and from then on I wanted to possess you more than anything in the world.'

'You gave up women?' she said sardonically, her eyes hardening in fury when he nodded with an air of aggrieved innocence. 'You're a liar!' she cried. 'Let's start with Josie!'

He leant on one elbow, his eyes solemn. 'Tell me something first. How did you get on the scene so quickly?'

She lowered her eyes but he tilted up her chin and forced her to look at him. Embarrassed, she mumbled her answer. 'She told me to wait on the balcony opposite and to come over when she walked into your flat.'

'Why?'

'She . . . she said I was crazy to trust you, that you'd go for any woman who was attractive enough,' she muttered, deeply ashamed.

'Exactly,' he said grimly. 'It was a set-up. That's all she did—walk in, drop her dress.'

'You were reaching out for her!'

'To pick up her dress,' he frowned. 'Ros, you fool! I was trying to catch the flight to Martinique! I had no time to take what Josie offered, even if I'd wanted to. If I make love to a woman, I like to do it properly. But I had more serious things on my mind. I was being accused of sharp practice, of fraud on a huge scale and all I wanted was to clear that up and then get back to the woman who'd given me paradise a few hours earlier. Do you think I'd jeopardise my relationship with you for a hasty tumble with one of your friends? Have some sense! There were plenty of willing women more discreet than Josie!'

She slid to the edge of the bed and slowly drew on her robe, going over what he'd said. 'I don't know...' She couldn't believe him, dared not. If she did, it meant she'd made a terrible mistake.

'You have more power to arouse me than any other woman,' he said softly. 'You know that.'

She looked at him and read his eyes, discovering a vulnerability in them that she'd not seen since they'd first met. And with a certainty that exploded in her head some of her assumptions about him were shattered into smithereens.

Yet...he'd married Annie. Her head lifted high on its slender neck. 'You can't have been serious about me—or you would never have married another woman,' she said quietly.

'I didn't love her, not then or at any other time,' he said with unnerving sincerity.

Rosalind clenched her hands till her nails dug into her palms. 'Not love her? Not ever?' she cried, aghast at what he was saying.

'You know what Annie's like,' he continued. 'She clings to her men like a limpet and makes them feel a heel for hurting her. Before my gaol term she'd been nothing more than my secretary—apart from the one night when she'd confronted me after you found me apparently reaching for Josie. You hurt me, Rosalind,' he said quietly.

Her jaw dropped. '*I* hurt *you*?' she said scornfully.

'You didn't trust me. You immediately jumped to the worst conclusions——'

'What should I have waited for, the video?' she said angrily. 'I believed the evidence of my own eyes,' she snapped. 'Nude woman, eager man. Not too hard to work that out.'

'You know,' he said cuttingly, 'your instincts are way off beam. You still haven't learnt to look further than the outside of people. OK, I'd had a good time playing the field in New Orleans when I first arrived. I'd had a brief affair with one of your friends and ditched her. But you should have known that my relationship with you was something else——'

'How could I know?' she cried in despair. 'I was inexperienced. You had one hell of a reputation——'

'You put your loyalty and belief in your friend Josie above anything we'd shared together. Didn't you realise she was doing her best to wreck our relationship?'

'Why would she do that?'

'Give me strength!' he muttered.

She coloured up. 'OK, so I'm naïve. Perhaps she was jealous, but I believed her because she was my friend, Chance. We'd been corresponding for years before I came to New Orleans—right from schooldays.'

'It doesn't mean you're honour bound to believe everything she says!' he said in exasperation. 'Both she and Annie were always jealous of you. You were not only more beautiful than they were, you had the kind of character and personality that they lacked.'

She blinked in surprise. That was news to her. 'They had more menfriends——'

'Rosalind, more men had *them*. It's not quite the same thing,' he drawled. 'They were popular because they slept around. Men who wanted sex didn't touch you. You were too far over their heads for them to do anything else but dream of such things. I wanted your untouched beauty.

I wanted to probe that serenity and bring you to life. But in doing so I woke the woman and she turned out to be as bitchy and as small-minded as the rest of them.'

'Thanks,' she said tightly. 'Wasn't I justified? Talk about off with the old and on with the new! You didn't take long to jump into Annie's arms for the consolation prize. Oh, I'm sorry!' she said, biting her lip at her shrewish outburst.

He smiled ruefully. 'No woman had ever rejected me before as you did. My pride was hurt enough to need a woman's voice telling me I was a terrific guy.' He gave a small snort of derision. 'There's insecure, immature youth for you. Look, at that age you cut your losses over your mistakes. I'd made a mistake in putting you on a pedestal. You fell off.'

'So Annie was nothing to you at all?' she asked quietly. 'Not ever?'

He inhaled with a vast gathering of breath. 'She stuck by me. While I was in prison, for the whole of those two years, she was my only contact with the outside world. For business reasons, no one knew I was there. People thought I was having a high old time. The reality was very different.' He came to sit beside her. 'I did a lot of thinking in prison,' he said grimly. 'About you and me.'

She froze and then half turned, meeting his storm-laden eyes warily. 'What... what about you and me?' she breathed.

'You women can't resist turning the knife,' he growled. 'Every single night, I lay awake thinking about what had happened between you and me and I swore that when I got out I was going to come and get you, Ros, and prove to you that what we had going between us was better than anything you'd ever get from anyone else—wherever you were, whatever you were doing, whoever you were with.'

Her world seemed to sink away from her feet. She clung to the rail frantically for support. No word of love, only possession, passion. But it would have been enough. If she'd known, she groaned, if he'd only written to tell her that, she would have been lifted from her terrible, mind-crippling depression in an instant. She wouldn't have needed time in a clinic. She could have continued to work then had her baby and waited for him and they would have been married.

CHAPTER EIGHT

ROSALIND felt sick to the pit of her stomach. If she'd known, Annie would never have offered to look after Melanie temporarily, to prevent Melly from being taken into care. At the time the offer had been a blessing. It had resulted in a nightmare.

'You were going to seek me out. What stopped you?' she asked, the despair making her sound sharp. She would not, could not meet his eyes any more.

'Annie met me with Melanie in her arms.'

'I see.' Her body was stiff and cold despite the sultry night, as if it had been frozen into ice. A terrible suspicion formed in her mind. 'Go on. What did she say?' she asked abruptly.

'Sweet and simple. "This is your child." '

She gritted her teeth to stop herself crying out in hopelessness. Annie had said Chance had jumped to conclusions about the child in her arms. That wasn't true. She'd *meant* Chance to think that the child was hers. Oh, Annie! she wailed to herself. Annie, you've betrayed me!

Rosalind began to tremble. Those letters she'd saved so carefully in the little cedar box, detailing her daughter's progress, all contained lies. Lies about Chance *assuming* Melly was Annie's daughter and his. Lies about how Annie had been incapable of telling him the truth because he had seemed so thrilled.

All that had led to a complicated web of untruth, with Annie's letters increasingly frantic as she had described the need to fool Chance. He'd had to believe Melly was a little younger than she really was. And, of course, there

171

had been the lie about the missing birth certificate, 'lost' during Annie's supposed stay with a relative in Senegal...

'You only married her out of duty,' she said harshly.

Rosalind tried to be reasonable, to be charitable. Annie had always longed to be married to someone rich and powerful but she was incapable of having children; the Decatur dynasty demanded heirs. It was the one factor that could have wrecked Annie's desperate, obsessive need for security in the form of rich, personable Chance.

And her friend had truly imagined that she'd been doing her a favour, by freeing her from the ties that a baby could bring. Rosalind had been so ill during her unhappy pregnancy that she'd been unable to work at all and had fallen into debt. Oh, she'd been persuaded that abandoning Melanie was the best thing for everyone concerned. Granted, she'd been able to build up her life after coming out of the clinic. But emotionally she'd been living in a desert.

Chance touched her arm and she jerked away sharply. Grimly he reached out and pulled her around to face him, tipping her chin up so that she couldn't avoid the dark black pools of treachery she'd fallen into so many times before.

'Do you think I shouldn't have married her?' he asked, glowering at her.

'Correct,' she whispered.

'I thought about it for a long time; don't think it was an easy decision. Would you prefer me to have rejected my own flesh and blood?' he demanded savagely. 'To say nothing of the woman who'd been more than loyal to me. That's more than I can say for you,' he said with a deep bitterness.

'Loyal?' she snapped. 'You think I should be loyal? To a cheat and a two-timing——'

'We've established that's not true, haven't we?'

She hung her head, racked by the terrible truth. Too late. It was all too late. 'Yes.'

'So you can imagine my rage when you wouldn't listen to any explanation. You made it quite clear you never wanted to see me again and I let my pride get in the way of clearing the air. Annie comforted me. I was furious with you and the world in general, singed, wounded and aching like hell, and she said I looked as if I needed the hair of the dog that bit me.'

'Please, no more!' whispered Rosalind. Waves of nausea churned in her stomach. She drove her teeth into her lip. 'Tell me about Martinique.'

His whole body tensed. Rosalind noticed that the hand resting on the bed was clenching and unclenching. 'I was shell-shocked when I came out of prison. I'd had everything worked out about you and me and I was looking forward to making a new start. It all seemed so simple. I'd find you and force you to believe me. That hope kept me going.'

'Oh,' she whispered. 'I can't bear to think of how you felt.'

'It turned me from a carefree young man into a robot,' he growled. 'Especially when I saw Annie with Melly tucked in her arms. She had never mentioned the fact that she was pregnant all the time she was writing to me in prison and telling me how the business was going. Then she went away to Senegal. I thought it was for a holiday from the strain of working so hard. Instead, it was to have her baby without anyone else knowing about it.'

Not Senegal, thought Rosalind. England. Annie had been getting acquainted with Melanie. And keeping her flat stomach from Chance's eyes.

'You didn't have to marry her,' she pointed out curtly. 'A settlement——'

'I had an ultimatum. Marriage, or no daughter,' he said quietly. Rosalind's heart went out to him, knowing how he must have felt, coming out of prison and finding himself in another, apparently of his own making. 'She said I'd never even have visiting rights with my record.'

Still she couldn't make eye contact. But she touched his hand and slowly it clasped hers. She knew how he'd felt. She'd been there. The depths of despair.

'Poor Annie. Now I understand why she couldn't bear to stay at the plantation any more. She'd used Melanie to——' Rosalind stopped just in time. He didn't know the whole truth.

'I never slept with her. Not ever,' he muttered. 'I couldn't. I don't know why. Hell. Yes, I do.'

He didn't elaborate. 'You didn't love her,' said Rosalind slowly. 'That's enough reason. Poor Annie. Poor Melly. She deserves a better life than the one she's had.'

'We must make it up to her,' he said softly.

'Yes,' she said, her eyes lifting to his. 'Oh, Chance!' she moaned, reaching for him.

He held her, warm, safe, comforting. And the love in her heart flowed out to him, bathing her in a healing glow. And then she felt his body move away and she didn't know why until she heard Melanie's relieved voice from the doorway.

'Oh, you're cuddlin'. I'm glad.'

Chance smiled tenderly at his daughter in her teddy-bear nightie. 'Sweetheart——'

'I came to say I was sorry to Ros,' she said uncertainly, looking from one to the other. Rosalind choked back a sob and held out her arms. Melanie flew to her. 'I was so *mad* with that Blanche,' wailed Melanie, curling up on the bed beside her. 'Daddy was just tellin' me about the wedding an' I was thinkin' how lovely it was an' along she came to spoil it all and they went back to the house so friendly... I thought I'd pick you some water hyacinths as a consolation an' worry Daddy a bit so he'd come lookin' but I got lost. I won't do it again. Games with people's feelings are stupid, aren't they?'

'Stupid,' she agreed, not meeting Chance's eyes. She and Josie had played a game and it had ruined her life. 'Don't ever fool around with emotions, Melanie, particularly where men are concerned. Be straight and honest all your life.'

'I will. Were you very upset, Ros?'

'Terribly,' she said shakily. 'I couldn't bear to think what had happened to you——'

'I was only missing a little while,' comforted Melanie. 'I knew Daddy would find me. It's his job to take care of us, you know. He lets himself get hurt, rather than me, you know. I'm glad you're going to be my mommy.'

'You—you have one,' she said croakily. 'What do you mean, he lets himself get hurt?'

'Oh, like when Mommy pushed Daddy down the stairs. He could've broken his fall if he'd wanted and saved himself but he chose to keep his arms round me so I'd be safe. Isn't that nice? All I got was bruises from where he gripped tight. He's awful strong,' she said admiringly. Rosalind looked at Chance for confirmation.

'You remember that, Melly?' he frowned. 'You were only three.'

'Sure I do.' She rubbed her eyes sleepily. 'Mommy was yellin' at you an' she lost her temper and pushed an' we fell. Then you went away forever, it seemed, an' when you came back I didn't like you because you were all hairy.'

'You screamed like a banshee at my beard,' he said softly.

'Why did you go away?' asked Rosalind huskily.

'I'd been in hospital with broken vertebrae and a broken neck. It was a long, endless flight of stairs,' he said ruefully.

'You had time to put out one hand to brace your fall and save yourself,' she breathed, full of admiration.

Chance gave a puzzled frown. 'But then I wouldn't have shielded Melanie's body completely and she would

have been hurt,' he reasoned, as if any man's natural
instinct would have been the same. 'The pain was nearly
as bad as discovering she was terrified of me. I had to
wear a supportive collar which had made it impossible
for me to shave. My daughter loathes beards to this day.'

'Mmm.' Melanie was almost asleep. 'You saved me,
though, didn't you? I worked that out later, of course.
I was too young then,' she explained sleepily to the open-
mouthed Rosalind.

Rosalind looked at Chance. 'That's why you lost
contact with your daughter,' she whispered. 'After saving
her life!'

'Poor kid! After the long period in hospital I was a
fearsome stranger with a mass of thick hair on his face,'
he said softly, his eyes on his slumbering daughter. Gently
he slipped the small thumb from her mouth and smiled
tenderly at the pouting lips.

'That must have hurt you.'

He gave a faint smile, but she could see the slicing
memory of pain that flickered over his eyes. 'She said I
was a nasty pirate, come to take her away.' He looked
across at Rosalind. 'Do you see why I was so upset when
she fell from the tree? I went into shock.'

'Oh, yes,' groaned Rosalind. 'You would have seen it
all happening again—your daughter falling, that awful
lurch in the stomach when something precious to you is
about to be hurt. I know what that's like,' she said
huskily, her gaze caressing him. 'Why did Annie push
you?'

He frowned. 'It was a kind of exasperated shove that
caught me off balance because Melly shifted her weight
at that moment. Not deliberate. I'd just told Annie that
our marriage wasn't working and we ought to part. She'd
accused me of being unfaithful and I'd picked Melanie
up to get her away. That made things worse, I think.
She'd imagined I'd take her own child from her! Can
you believe it?'

'Oh, yes. I can,' she said, sorry for Annie, under-standing her insecurity and realising that Annie's deceit had rebounded on her with a vengeance. 'She's put you through hell, hasn't she?' said Rosalind quietly.

'Nearly as much as you have,' he said quietly.

He rolled off the bed and took Melanie back to her room while Rosalind sat motionless with shock. Hell? What had she done to deserve that remark? Surely an unreasonable obsession couldn't match what Annie had done to him.

Chance returned and stood in the doorway, brooding. 'I'm sorry I ripped open your dress and frightened you,' he muttered. 'I was beside myself with anger and I lost control. For the first time in my life, I didn't know what I was doing. I don't hurt defenceless people.'

She hesitated for a moment before she spoke, but this was a time for being truthful about feelings. 'I doubt your victims in Martinique would believe that,' she re-minded him quietly.

'That was a mistake. My manager was to blame. He'd worked the fraud and let me take the rap,' he said harshly. 'He's now in prison himself. My lawyers have just accepted an out-of-court settlement in compen-sation for wrongful arrest and unnecessary suffering.' He gave a short, humourless laugh. 'As if anything can compensate for what I've been through!'

Rosalind felt all the breath leave her body. He'd been misjudged by everyone, perhaps because he appeared to have everything and some people wanted a share, while others were jealous and were glad to see him spit-roasted. She groaned. It would have been wonderful if they'd been able to love one another without these terrible years remorselessly tearing them apart.

'We'll try,' she said shakily. 'We'll make a good mar-riage for all our sakes. I'm glad your record has been wiped clean.'

He smiled thinly—not the response she expected at all—and lightly kissed the top of her head. 'Pity it's left such a scar,' he said in a low tone. 'I doubt I can be completely trusting again. Sleep well.'

Rosalind put all her energies into making him—and Melanie—happy. Sometimes she thought he was behaving in a carefree manner, but then a shadow came over his face and she wanted to run to him and throw her arms around him, telling him it was all right, he was loved very deeply.

But she was prevented by the dark brooding of his eyes on her, accusing and resentful, as if suspicious of her motives. Plans for the wedding went ahead and Rosalind told herself that it would take time for him to trust her, as it had taken time for her to trust him.

Annie wrote to them and Chance went to see her in Atlanta, reporting that she was happy and in love and wanted to keep in touch. But she was adamant that she wanted to give up all rights to Melanie and Chance just couldn't understand that.

'She's the child's mother, for God's sake!' He glared at Rosalind as they sat one night on the gallery having a drink after dinner. 'It beats me how a woman can separate herself from her child. Surely there's a never-ending emotional tie?'

Rosalind silently sipped her brandy, keeping her lashes lowered. If she defended Annie, her own raw nerve-endings would be too apparent. 'Don't be hard on her. It makes the situation easier for us. Please. I don't want to discuss it.'

'I do,' he frowned. 'Would *you* hand over your child——?'

'Please!' she snapped. And clenched her jaw to control herself. That had been too loud, too vehement; Chance was looking at her very curiously. 'It won't help to keep going over it,' she said shakily. Her hand shook as it reached for the glass.

He caught her wrist and laid her hand on his, seeing how badly it trembled. His eyes were black and unfathomable, the tension in his body threatening and filling her with alarm.

No, she moaned to herself, her eyes shutting out the sight of his frighteningly savage expression. He *mustn't* find out. Not when we're on the brink of happiness.

'Rosalind,' he said with soft menace. 'Why won't you talk about it?' he demanded. 'What's making you shiver with fear?'

'Perhaps I've got...' Her voice trailed into nothing. No. She wouldn't pretend she had flu. There ought to be no more pretending. Her whole body shuddered at the thought of telling him.

The hand that gripped hers tightened until she wanted to scream with pain. Her eyes opened to plead with him but she saw only a cruel determination etched into Chance's handsome features.

'Tell me what I need to know,' he grated, his eyes flashing dangerously. 'Before we marry. I have a right to know what I'm taking on. And what there is in your past that I should know about.'

Rosalind drew in a jagged breath that did little to ease the tightness in her chest. He'd never trust her again; he'd be angry and despise her for giving up her child. He'd cancel the marriage, forbid her to see Melanie...

'Owww!' she groaned, wincing at the pressure on her hand.

Chance stood up, a forbidding figure in the light of the gas-lamps, dark shadows playing on the planes of his face and making the hunch of his broad shoulders very intimidating.

'Tell me,' he said, softness overlying steel.

'You're not going to like this,' she said dully.

'I imagined as much.'

She saw the flare of cruelty in his eyes and flinched. 'It's—it's about the reason for my depression.' She couldn't go on. His eyebrow had lifted cynically. 'You're making it difficult,' she complained.

'Perhaps because I have a feeling this is going to alter things between us,' he said harshly. 'Am I right?' She nodded miserably. 'Then get on with it. I like my medicine neat.'

She watched him fill his glass with brandy and down it in one gulp. He was as nervous as she was. He didn't want things to change either. With a supreme effort, she blurted out the truth. 'I was depressed because I was unhappy our relationship had foundered and . . . and because I was ill. I was pregnant.'

There was a breathless hush. Chance didn't move for several seconds though there were raging fires in his dark eyes. He appeared to have stopped breathing. 'Pregnant.' She nodded apprehensively. 'My God!' he whispered, appalled.

'That—that's why I was upset when you wanted me to stay at the plantation because Annie was taking herself off to the clinic,' she said tremulously.

His face was haggard. 'Of course. I understand. You wouldn't want to stay.' He seemed to struggle with himself and when he spoke it was in a cracked, dry voice. 'I suggest——' He strode over the boards to the up-river door, pausing in the doorway, his stiff neck and hunched shoulders intimidatingly tense. 'I suggest we end this engagement immediately and I get you on the next plane home.'

With a hoarse cry, Rosalind scrambled to her feet, sending her chair flying. 'Oh, I was afraid of this!' she cried in distress. 'You'd deny me my child?'

'What are you talking about?' he snarled, whirling around. 'I'm telling you to leave me——'

'And Melanie!' she wailed.

'How many kids do you want? You have your own damn child!' he roared. 'That's where you belong—with him, or her! Go back to your brat. Go back to Tom, or whoever the father is. If you think——'

'Wait a cotton-pickin' moment!' she yelled. 'You haven't understood! Tom is nothing to me; he never has been. He was the boss of the agency where I worked and that's all. I'm talking about Melanie! Melanie's my child! I don't have any other, only Melanie!'

'She's mine!' he roared.

'*And mine,*' Rosalind whispered.

The big body rocked. Two fists grabbed the door-jamb and then Chance hovered there unsteadily, his eyes glowing with an unholy fire. '*No*! By God!' he cried hoarsely. 'You think to take my child from me? She's Annie's! I saw her as a little baby in Annie's arms! What are you trying to do to me? Don't you think I've been through enough agony?'

Rosalind looked at his harrowed face with pity. 'Oh, yes, I do. But I swear she's mine, Chance. *My* baby.' Her voice softened, wishing he wasn't taking this so badly, wishing she could ease his pain. 'Don't you know a mother's love when you see it?'

'But it's impossible...' He shook his head as if to clear his brain from cobwebs.

'I had a terrible pregnancy because I was distraught about you,' she said in the cold, icy silence. Her voice trembled from the ferocity of his fevered eyes. 'I loved you so much. I suffered too, Chance! I cried more nights than I care to remember!'

'I don't believe this——' he began harshly.

'You must,' she said piteously. 'You must understand how it came about.'

'I'm riveted,' he grated with cruel sarcasm.

She ignored it, too determined to come clean. 'I couldn't hold any job down when I was carrying my baby, I was in such a state. Sick, sleepless from crying, desolate... I didn't want to eat and I lost weight. I caught every virus going. I drifted from one flat to another——'

'What about your parents?' he asked abruptly.

'You know the situation there. I couldn't go to them,' she said stiffly. 'I was too ashamed, my stepmother disliked me, my father never cared much.'

She saw he was just standing there with total disapproval in his expression and she knew she'd lost him forever. Her body slumped and her voice grew listless as she dragged the story out from inside her. He would hear her out. And then she'd leave. A ragged sob shuddered from her body.

'Go on,' he said without expression or pity.

She swallowed, feeling as nauseous as when she'd carried her beloved child. 'When—when Melanie was born,' she said in a half-whisper, 'I had postnatal depression. They put me in a clinic. They wanted to put my baby into a children's home and I knew they meant to foster her out. She was all I had of you and I wanted to keep her. I wrote to Annie in despair and she offered to look after her. Melly is mine. I have the birth certificate.'

'Yours. Yours.' He shook his head slowly, as if her words were just beginning to reach his brain. 'Yours!' he exploded. 'My God! You pretend that you love children, yet you gave up your *child*? Your own child?'

She gulped at the distrust in his black eyes. 'No, I didn't, it happened!' she said hysterically.

'It happened?' he scorned, his lip curled in contempt. 'Something like that doesn't just *happen*.'

'It did! Annie can't have children!' yelled Rosalind, her need to keep Melanie this time greater than her loyalty. The words spilled out, tumbling in wild disorder, released from where they'd been dammed up for so long. 'She saw her chance. She used Melanie to get you. She did, because she knew you needed children and you wouldn't marry her if she was barren and she believed truly that I'd be better off without Melanie so she thought it would be all right because it meant she could be your wife and have a home and a family and that's been her dearest wish ever since we were children together. She saw her chance to have her dream of security and she took it. Oh, God!' she cried. 'She took my baby! She thought she was acting in my interests and hers! I was ill, drugged, half out of my mind! I wasn't part of that conspiracy, I swear it; you have to believe that. I couldn't intentionally abandon my child.' She raised her desperate face to his. 'You know what I feel for Melanie! You know I love her more than my life!'

'You could have done something when you recovered,' he snapped.

'It was too late by then. Annie had sent an avalanche of ecstatic letters telling me how wonderful life was, how happy Melanie seemed. I struggled with my conscience and bowed to the inevitable.' Rosalind mechanically uprighted the chair and slumped down into it.

'You said nothing, gave no hint, all this time,' he said harshly, his eyes two black furnaces of anger.

'I couldn't, don't you understand, you fool?' she cried in exasperation. 'I loved my child too much to break up what I fondly thought was a happy home. Happy home!' she laughed, on the brink of losing control. 'When all the time you and Annie were not in love at all and were starving her of affection! Oh, if I'd *known*!' she growled, full of bitterness. 'I would have walked across the Atlantic to get her back! How do you think I managed to survive all these years knowing someone else had tricked me into surrendering my child? I closed my heart, that's what I did. You know what that's like. You did the same when you had to adjust to marrying Annie even though you didn't love her. You closed your heart when you believed Melanie would never be part of you. Have pity for me, Chance!'

But he made no attempt to comfort her or placate her at all. Finally he spoke in a hoarse, slow whisper.

'You gave your child to Annie and she brought her to me. Dear heaven! I can hardly believe it!' He passed a hand through his hair, tousling it into an untidy tumble. 'When I saw Annie with a baby in her arms,' he rasped, 'and she said Melanie was mine, it crossed my mind that I might not be the father. After all, I'd only made love to her once. Then I saw how much Melly resembled me at that age.'

'So you believed her,' she said dully.

'I did. But,' he said in a shaking voice, his eyes flashing dangerously, 'I never, ever dreamed that the woman who *held* my child might not be the *mother*!'

There was horror on his face. Horror and rage. He turned his head to one side. As if he couldn't bear to look at her any more he shut his eyes, his body shaking with emotion, lost in his own world as he tried to come to terms with the destruction of his life by a lie.

Appalled at his reaction, Rosalind bowed to the inevitable. The relationship between them would never work now he felt such contempt for her. And she wasn't going to subject her daughter to the strain of two adults fighting a cold battle over her head. Chance would meet someone, some day he could properly love. He had so much to give. Till then, Melly was better off with one loving parent.

She silently rose, slipped off her ring and laid it without a sound on the table. Then she walked like a zombie along the gallery and down the steps, not noticing the torrential rain until she was halfway across the lawn and her feet were squelching in the steaming mud.

She ran for the trees and leaned against the rough bark wearily, coming to terms with her desolate future. Huge drops fell on her upturned, pale face from the dripping leaves and they mingled with her tears.

If she packed now, she thought, trying to get the rags of her mind together, she could leave straight away and wait in the airport.

A huge gasping sob of angry frustration welled from her body. 'Chance!' she moaned into the darkness. 'Chance,' she whispered. 'Chance, I love you.'

Her numbed brain suddenly registered the sound of splashing, and Chance's shout. He sounded like a raging bull. He was coming to exact his revenge on her, she thought hysterically, all reason flying away. Without thinking, she began to run. The sound of his heavy breathing came closer.

'Rosalind!' he was roaring.

'No, no!' she screamed, ploughing her way through mud, finding her shoes had stuck. Frantically she wrenched free and ran on barefoot.

Suddenly he cannoned into her with a thud that took her breath away and they went flying, landing with an agonising crash on the grass, the rain and mud splattering her face and choking her. She rolled over and he grabbed her just as sheet lightning lit him, its searing light revealing a face surrounded in hot steaming air and so energised with anger that Rosalind gave a sharp, strangled scream at the sight and tried to wriggle away, beside herself with fear.

'Where the—devil do you—think you're—going?' he yelled, incapable of normal speech with the rain cascading down his glistening face so relentlessly that it took his breath away.

'I—don't know!' she spluttered, feeling stupid, half drowning in the wall of water crashing down on them. 'Anywhere,' she gasped. 'Anywhere—away—from you.'

'You've been—running for—too long.' He sucked in a breath and dashed a hand over his dripping lashes, gasping the words out between gulps of air and choking water. 'You'll damn—well stay and—accept—responsibilities.'

'Stay?' she gasped, swallowing warm water. 'But—I thought—you were furious—horrified!'

'Yes! With Annie!' he yelled. 'She cheated me of you!' He paused for breath, his chest heaving. 'I was horrified. God, what you went through!'

The skin of her face felt pink and stinging from the driving rain. She pushed her hands into the muddy ground, to raise herself, and found her hand almost covered in water. She was being submerged, she thought wildly. Drowned and clutching at straws. She must have imagined that he'd sounded sorry for her.

Impatiently he thrust her back down and the water lapped over her face with the sudden movement and then stayed at the level of her ear. 'Melanie loves you...I love you,' he shouted, heedless of the tempest above them. 'For her sake——'

There seemed to be a turmoil in her head as frenzied as the one around them. 'Did—did you say—you loved me?' she choked. Stunned, she put her hand up to his hair, which was plastered in black curls over his forehead, the deluge of water streaming down from him to her. He tried to shield her with his body, and she found some respite from the downpour. 'No,' she cried. 'You don't have to pretend any more——'

'Who's pretending?' he growled. 'I've loved you— since you were—eighteen years old...' Rosalind lifted her arms to protect his head from the rain, screwing up her eyes so that she could see his face through the screen of giant pearly raindrops on her lashes. 'I've ached. And hungered. For longer than I care to recall. Time doesn't heal. People are wrong. I stayed in love. The wound got deeper. Don't listen to what I say, don't pay any attention to the words, look at me, read my eyes, damn you, and start discovering the facts of life,' he said passionately.

'Oh, Chance!' she choked, the tears coursing down her face and being lost in the rain. 'You love me!'

'Madly. Come out of the rain——'

'Oh, Chance! This is wonderful! So wonderful that it's sunny!' she grinned in delight. 'The sun's shining.'

He turned his head slightly and was sluiced in sheets of rain. 'You're crazy!' he yelled, gasping for breath. 'It's chucking—it down!'

'It's shining,' she insisted blissfully, giggling at his amazed expression. 'Look, if we wriggle—we'll be beneath Oak Alley. Shelter there. I love you.' She nuzzled her wet face into his chest. 'I love you,' she mumbled, her mouth full of soaking shirt. 'I love you,' she breathed, her mouth full of his. 'Hold me.'

'What?'

She began to squeal as he rolled with her in the mud, over and over, till they had reached the relative shelter of the trees.

'You look disgustingly grubby!' he laughed, his eyes alight with exhilaration.

'Someone will have to clean me up,' she said smugly. He laughed again, and the elemental wildness of their surroundings matched the unbridled joy inside her.

'Steam cleaning's my specialty,' he grinned. 'I begin here...' he kissed along the line of her hair '...and I end here...' He sucked her toes and she gave a little squeal.

'When do we get to the bit in between?' she asked demurely.

'Any minute now. First, put my ring back on. I want to marry you so badly. And then I want to hold you,' he said huskily as he slid the ring on to her finger. 'I want to hold you so tight that you'll know I'll never let you go.'

'Could make shaving tricky,' she laughed, her fingers rubbing on his burgeoning stubble. 'Your daughter and I don't like beards.'

'Don't you want to cut my throat with a razor any more?' he murmured, nuzzling her ear.

'Brave, wasn't I?' she giggled.

'Foolhardy. You don't know what control I had to exercise to prevent the first sexual assault in a barber's chair that New Orleans has ever known,' he grinned. She laughed in delight and he smiled at her contentedly. 'It's a long time since I was happy,' he said softly. 'How about a little alligator wrassling?'

'One hold, two submissions?' she suggested.

'A thousand holds. Wait till I show you. But you got the submission bit right. I love you,' he said tenderly. '*I love you.*'

'Can you love me till dawn?' she murmured, languorously moving beneath him in the steamy warmth of the night.

'Forever,' he whispered. 'I can love you forever.'

HARLEQUIN®

PRESENTS *Plus*

It wasn't the best start to a working relationship:
Debra's private detective sister had asked her to spy on
Marsh Graham—Debra's new boss! But if Debra began
by believing Marsh had suspicious motives, she soon
realized that, when it came to her, Marsh had desires of
a more personal kind....

Was Denzil Black moving from woman to woman, seducing them, then leaving them drained and helpless? Clare
thought of Denzil as a vampire lover...so when she realized that she was next on his list of conquests, she
resolved that *Denzil* would learn what it was to be a victim of love!

In Presents Plus, there's more to love....

Watch for:

A Matter of Trust by Penny Jordan
Harlequin Presents Plus #1719

and

Vampire Lover by Charlotte Lamb
Harlequin Presents Plus #1720

Harlequin Presents Plus
The best has just gotten better!

Available in February, wherever Harlequin books are sold.

Fifty red-blooded, white-hot, true-blue hunks
from every State in the Union!

Look for MEN MADE IN AMERICA! Written by some
of our most popular authors, these stories feature some
of the strongest, sexiest men, each from a different state
in the union!

Two titles available every month at your favorite
retail outlet.

In January, look for:

WITHIN REACH by Marilyn Pappano (New Mexico)
IN GOOD FAITH by Judith McWilliams (New York)

In February, look for:

THE SECURITY MAN by Dixie Browning
(North Carolina)
A CLASS ACT by Kathleen Eagle
(North Dakota)

You won't be able to resist MEN MADE IN AMERICA!